THE CITADEL OF WHISPERS

THE CITADEL OF WHISPERS

CHOOSE YOUR OWN ADVENTURE®

KAZIM ALI

CHOOSECO
WAITSFIELD, VERMONT

Book design: Peter Holm, Sterling Hill Productions

For information regarding permission, write to:

CHOOSECO

P.O. Box 46
Waitsfield, Vermont 05673
www.cyoa.com

Publisher's Cataloging-In-Publication Data
(Prepared by The Donohue Group, Inc.)

Names: Ali, Kazim, 1971- author. | Alemanno, Andrea, illustrator. |
    Muddy, Iris, illustrator.
Title: The Citadel of Whispers / Kazim Ali.
Other Titles: Choose your own adventure.
Description: Waitsfield, Vermont : Chooseco, [2021] | Interest age level: 012-
    017. | Summary: "You were only ten years old when the Whisperers came to
    your village looking for candidates. Their identity, like their work, is
    secret and unknown to most of the people who live in Elaria, a mountainous
    land of difficult terrain surrounded by vast oceans that few, if any, have
    crossed. You, Krishi, were tapped by a man disguised as a peddler and poet
    to join the Whisperers at the Citadel, and train in their arts of magic and
    combat. You are still new in your training when a mysterious new student
    arrives in the port, bringing with him news of imminent war."--Provided by
    publisher.
Identifiers: ISBN 9781937133924
Subjects: LCSH: Apprentices--Juvenile fiction. | Magic--Juvenile fiction. | Com-
    bat--Juvenile fiction. | Imaginary places--Juvenile fiction. | Imaginary wars
    and battles--Juvenile fiction. | CYAC: Apprentices--Fiction. | Magic--Fic-
    tion. | Combat--Fiction. | Imaginary places--Fiction. | Imaginary wars and
    battles--Fiction. | LCGFT: Fantasy fiction. | Choose-your-own stories.
        Classification: LCC PZ7.A39688 Ci 2021 | DDC [Fic]--dc23

Published simultaneously in the United States and Canada

Printed in the United States

10 9 8 7 6 5 4 3 2 1

IN THE BEGINNING

Elaria is a vast land, surrounded by wide oceans. It is your home, and it is home to the Whisperers.

Eastern Elaria is made up of many small city-states. Their capitals are ruled by local princes, who are elected by the people. Each city protects the towns and villages around it.

The middle of the continent is bisected by an impassable mountain range. To the west of the mountains lies the mighty Narbolin Empire. In the old times, the West—like the East—was also made up of small states, each with an elected ruler-prince.

But the major port city of the west, Narbolis, slowly accumulated wealth, power, and influence. It conquered the smaller states one by one. Today, a dynasty of emperors rule. Their lineage is by bloodline, not election, and they rule for life.

For hundreds of years, peace has been kept throughout both the city-states of eastern Elaria and the Narbolin Empire by the Whisperers. The Whisperers are a shadowy order of diplomats, spies, and scholars who work toward harmony and maintain the balance of power in the realm. Most of the common people of the realm don't even know the Whisperers exist!

In this book, YOU are Krishi, a young student in the fabled Citadel of Whispers. The Citadel is kept safe on a volcanic archipelago off the southern coast of Elaria. Whisperers are found in all kingdoms of Elaria. They hide in plain sight in various secret outposts. A small group of thirty or forty always live in the Citadel. Some are wise teachers, but most are the students who are there to learn the disciplines of the order—diplomacy, combat, spy work, and various schools of magic.

You and your friends Zara and Saeed have lived together in the Citadel for four years and are now preparing for your first tests and trials as you become Whisperers.

CYREN

NARBO
EMPI

Narbolis

KULS

equator

THE PIRATE
ISLES

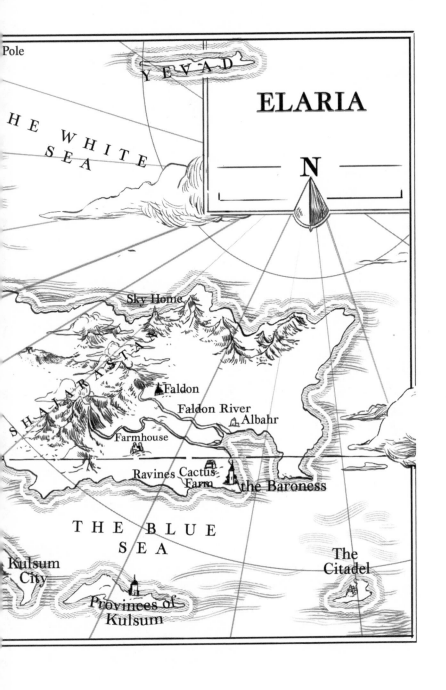

LIST OF CHARACTERS

AT THE CITADEL

Students
YOU are Krishi, a junior student
Saeed, a junior student
Zara, a junior student
Pedro, a junior student
Dimple, a younger student
  Masters
Chandh Sahib, the principal master
Sandhya, the weapons master
Suraj, the dance master
  Visitors
Arjun, a prospective student
Dev Acharya, a Whisperer

AT THE FARMHOUSE

Shivani, the principal master
The Colonel, Shivani's secretary
Rabab, the language and diplomacy master

AT THE CACTUS FARM

Rubio and Meghan, prickly-pear cactus farmers
Tommy, their elder son
Max, their younger son
Doron, Casey, Finnegan, Alec, and Caleb,
  workers at the farm

AT THE MANOR HOUSE

Lowelia, the Baroness of the Two Rivers
    district
Javid, her castellan
Margalit, boss of the garden crew
Etheldreda, a gardener
The Duc de Berry, a member of the Guild
    Council
The Countess of South Cliff, a member of the
    Guild Council
The Marquis de Bois, a member of the Guild
    Council
The Dazzling Zubaydah, an entertainer
Dannel, one of the Baroness's guards

IN ALBAHR

Bobby, Robert, and Roberto, the proprietors of
    The Three Roberts

SOME PIRATES

Zephyr, a scoundrel
Dalilah, the Duchess of Kulsum and Captain of
    the Blade
Nakul and Sahadev, two sailors

INTRODUCTION

You ou were only ten years old when the Whisperers came to your village. Most people don't even know the Whisperers exist. Whisperers come and go in secret. They scout the entire realm for candidates, and their processes are mysterious and selective. When a candidate is identified, the parents of the child are negotiated with directly.

In your case, it was Chandh Sahib who came to the village himself, disguised as a peddler of pots and pans. He was in the kitchen of your family's modest house, speaking with your parents. Suddenly he threw off the coarse over-jacket he wore and stood up, revealing a robe of black velvet with sigils of a silver moon in all its phases stitched down the sides.

"What is this?" your father exclaimed, though your mother seemed unsurprised.

"The secret is this," Chandh Sahib said. "I represent the Whisperers, an order devoted to keeping peace in the land. We work in secret and would like to take Krishi to our school for training. We will send you money to support your family and the village, and Krishi will come back to see you once a year. None of this must be known by anyone."

You were intrigued and excited but worried your father would object. Then your mother put her hand on his. He looked over at her.

"Do you remember when I told you I had traveled across the continent in my youth?" she asked him.

He nodded.

She reached to her neck and pulled a medallion up from under her tunic. It glinted bright silver—a small crescent moon. Chandh Sahib wears an amulet just like it, but while his depicts a full moon, your mother's depicts the new crescent.

"Sister," said Chandh Sahib, nodding toward her. "I did not recognize you."

"We appear as we wish to be seen," she said, as if repeating a line she had long studied.

And so it was. You were given your *own* amulet depicting the first crescent of the moon, and you left your family and crossed the water to the Isle of the Citadel, where the ancient and infamous Citadel of Whispers is perched.

You still returned home every summer, as Chandh Sahib promised, but as the years passed, whenever you were home in your village, you found yourself longing for the twisting mountain trails and deep forested interior of the mysterious Isle of the Citadel.

In those first, heady days, you and your best friends Zara and Saeed spent countless hours exploring the labyrinthine passages of the Citadel itself, but your favorite times were when you wandered alone, climbing high into the ramparts which overlooked the ocean, or else following the maze of paths deep into the woods where other and more ancient buildings of the Whisperers were rumored to be.

SECTION 1

"Get up, Krishi! I barely landed that kick!"

You are flat on your back, shaking your head and staring up at the main ceiling of the Great Hall in the Citadel of Whispers. The ceiling is painted a dark night-blue, and silver stars sparkle in the shapes of constellations. Or are you just seeing stars because Zara hit you so hard?

"Whoa," you say, propping yourself up on your elbows and grinning at Zara, who is still in fighting stance. "That was a good one!"

Sandhya, the tall and imposing Whisperer who has been teaching the unarmed combat class, glides into view. Like all of you, she is wearing a long and tightly corseted dress, hardly the normal gear for engaging in fisticuffs. Her amulet, depicting a half-moon, hangs just below her throat.

"While I wanted all of you to learn the art of fighting in restrictive clothing, Krishi, the point was not to learn how to *take* a hit!"

"Sorry, master," you say, ducking your head in contrition

and fumbling your way to your feet. The clothing you wear is both heavy and unwieldy. "Master," you say, summoning up your courage, "why would we be wearing heavy dresses like this one when we fight?"

Sandhya arches one eyebrow and casts a cold eye around the giggling students who have gathered, silencing everyone without a word. How does she do that?

"A fight you can plan is easy to win," she says. "It is when you are completely unprepared that you must learn. Saeed! Front and center. Let's see if you can do better than your friend."

Saeed shuffles into the center of the group. You make a little face of entreaty at Zara, silently asking her to go easy on Saeed. Zara smirks at you and you're not sure if she understood you. You, Zara, and Saeed all started at the Citadel as students together, and you feel protective of Saeed, who has never excelled at the physical training which all Whisperers must undergo. It doesn't help that Zara is easily the best fighter in the class.

"Assume your stance," instructs Sandhya, and Zara crouches low, her arms raised, the left out in front and the right pulled back toward her body. Saeed sighs, and then crouches in some approximation of Zara's fighting stance, but looser. Zara looks like a coiled animal ready to strike, while Saeed looks like a noodle that is about to collapse. "Wait!" Sandhya strides over to Saeed, reaches over, and pulls out the long wooden hairpin from his bun. The cinch clatters to the ground and his curls fall into his eyes.

"Teacher Sandhya, why?" Saeed cries out, and you are indignant on his behalf. He was already at a disadvantage against Zara, whose hair is still tightly bound in the bun and hairpin that all Whisperers wear.

"You must be ready for any circumstance," Sandhya says silkily. "Now, fight!"

As soon as she says the word, Zara springs forward toward Saeed. Then the unexpected happens. You catch the quickest flash of a crafty look on Saeed's little face and then he drops to the ground. That's why he was so loose. Zara's mouth forms a little "o" of surprise and she tries to correct herself, but Saeed is already kicking out. His heel strikes the back of Zara's knee and she goes down, tangled in her skirts. Saeed rolls over quickly. He punches out from the ground, catching Zara lightly on the side of her head.

Zara rolls with the punch and laughs at Saeed.

"You'll have to hit harder than that to knock me down!"

She pushes herself onto her hands and knees, but Saeed is already spinning on his knees. He braces himself on one elbow and gives her a second hard kick. Zara collapses again. The students cheer. You cheer too. You never get to see Zara take a licking.

"Well done," Sandhya says, nodding her head in approval.

"Why anyone wears these things is beyond me!" Zara exclaims with relief as she wriggles out of her heavy, structured dress at the end of class, pulling on the plain linen tunic and pants that every student at the Citadel wears.

"I don't know," says Saeed, "something about the corset made it easier to kick out at you. I think it held my posture."

Zara rolls her eyes. "Something only a boy would say. You're lucky you'll never have to wear one of these in regular life."

"Unless we're on a mission," you say, slowly realizing why Sandhya would train you to fight in these clothes. "I mean, we all have to grow our hair at least to our shoulders, right? Working in disguise is part of our training. The clothes we wear are part of that too."

Zara makes a face. "I wonder what Chandh Sahib has in mind for our first mission?"

And then, as if by mentioning his name Zara summoned him, Chandh Sahib appears at the doors to the Great Hall.

He is a small and slender man with pale skin and bright silver hair, which—like all Whisperers' hair—is shoulder length, though, unlike all of yours, his hair is loose and unbound.

"My students," he calls, clapping his hands. "The final period of classes today is canceled. We have special visitors at the Citadel tonight and we will need everyone's help preparing the meal. Report to your respective work duties."

"Whoa," Saeed says. He pauses, watching Sandhya and Chandh Sahib talk quietly to each other as the rest of your friends file past. "I wonder who's coming?"

"Who cares," Zara says, twisting a lock of hair in her finger. "I had dance last. Good on me for not having to learn that stupid choreo Suraj is trying to teach us. What about you, Krishi?"

"My work duty is at the docks!" you say with a grimace. You have to report to the docks at the large cave at the foot of the hill.

You race down the one hundred and eight—you know because you counted—steps that lead from the main Citadel to the cave and past the giant tapestry. It hangs to the right of the stairwell and depicts the Citadel under attack. An armada is gathered at the base. On the ramparts, Whisperers fling fire down upon them. The great beacon at the pinnacle of the Citadel is lit, and its angry orange flames lick the purple sky.

"This image is a reminder," Chandh Sahib said when he showed you the tapestry during a history lecture, "that the Whisperers exist to preserve the peace but that times were not always peaceful."

"Will we have to fight again?" Saeed asked, his eyes wide with fear.

Chandh Sahib waved a dismissive hand. "You are safe here in the Citadel, though it would be most dangerous should an enemy find their way inside. Great are the secrets the Citadel guards, and mighty are the ancient magics that lie dormant here."

"Magic?" Saeed asked, his eyes now filling with wonder and maybe a little bit of greed. "Can you teach us?"

"Magic is the name we give to unspeakably powerful forces; a human on their own could not access it; the most powerful magic must be channeled through powerful objects meant for such purposes, like the Heart of the Storm, the great rock temple in the center of our island. But sometimes a smaller form can be drawn from the environment around you. In this case, the Whisperers were drawing energy from the storm and from the beacon above the Citadel to create the fire. But that is a lesson for another time."

"But you said we had to be prepared for anything," Saeed protested.

"Magic cannot be taught," Chandh Sahib explained patiently. "It comes only from self-knowledge. Those who use it for personal gain are easily corrupted. Use of magic comes from your own natural awareness of your own body, your mind, and the unspeakable spirit within. It comes from *practice* and *study*, not from need or want. Let us instead talk of the Treaty of Two Rivers and how it came to benefit the cactus farmers of the Everest Canyons . . ."

The memory of Chandh Sahib lecturing captures you for a moment. The taskmaster is quick to interrupt and bring you back to reality.

He assigns you your work, and you are still sweeping when you hear the dock master cry out. A sleek galleon appears at the tidal wall, mooring at the breakline. A longboat is lowered down so that passengers can come into harbor.

The ship bears no emblem, only a black flag with a scarlet border. *Pirates?* Being given safe harbor here in the Citadel? Who *are* these visitors for whom classes were canceled and the entire Citadel put to work?

The sailors call out from the deck and throw the heavy lines from the ship. The dockhands collect the lines and knot them around the metal cleats on the dock so the boat is secured.

A gangplank lowers and the passengers disembark. The Captain is an older-than-middle-aged woman dressed in breeches and a claret waistcoat. She shouts orders from the aft deck.

You watch as a stern and dour-looking man leads a sullen youth close to your age down the gangplank.

The old man's face is haggard, with deep frown lines. Though his hair is cropped close to his scalp, he too wears an amulet as Whisperers do, though his depicts a crescent reversed—the old moon.

The boy who follows looks nothing like him, but he is also frowning. His hair is long, like the Whisperers, and his eyes are rimmed dark with kohl. Is he a Whisperer too? If he is wearing an amulet, you cannot see it, as he is wrapped fully against the cold. If he *is* one, you imagine he would be happier to arrive to the Citadel.

As if hearing your thoughts, the older man stops walking. His eyes cast over the docks and suddenly fix on you. *Can he read my mind?* you wonder. Suddenly the slightest ghost of a smile appears on his cadaverous face.

You start, and turn back to your sweeping in earnest. The older man gestures the youth forward and they mount the stairs to the Citadel. When you try to sneak another look, the old man looks back at you with a mysterious expression on his face.

"What do you think is going on?" Zara asks you as you stand together at the long table, waiting for the masters to sit. Zara is ace at the technique of speaking with her mouth closed, her lips not moving a millimeter. "And who is that little snit?" She tilts her head in the most minuscule way toward the boy who arrived on the ship, sitting next to the older man.

"No idea," you say back through gritted teeth, though you feel your lips quiver a little as you say it.

"I heard it's a new student," says Saeed, enthusiastically, not bothering to try to be stealthy. "And you know who that is, right? It's Dev Acharya, one of the most senior Whisperers on the continent. He was Chandh Sahib's *teacher*."

You look over at the man with new interest. He sits to the left of Chandh Sahib, who is standing at the head of the table.

The boy, looking bored and distracted, sits across from Dev Acharya, to Chandh Sahib's right. He does not make eye contact with anyone, even Dev Acharya.

Dev Acharya's hair, unlike the hair of every other Whisperer you have ever known, is cropped close to his head. His deep-set dark eyes rove around the room and never settle. You do not want him to catch you looking at him again, so you look down at the plate of vegetables which is now being passed along the table. As everyone serves themselves, Chandh Sahib sits. That's the signal for everyone besides your guests to finally be seated.

The meal passes without further event. Every once in a while, you steal a look over at Dev Acharya, and every single time his eyes flick to you from whomever he is talking to. After a while it becomes a game. You should know better; he's an advanced Whisperer. You'll never catch him unaware, but you can't help yourself. He speaks with Chandh Sahib alone throughout the meal, and his young charge, bored by whatever conversation they are having, eats his meal in silence.

"What is he thinking?" Zara asks. "The boy. Read him, Krishi. You're the best at reaching out."

You put your fork down and focus on the boy's face. You try, as you've learned in your lessons, to travel past what you see and into his thoughts.

"He's bored," you say.

Zara blows air out of her lips. "Anyone can see that," she says. "You don't have to be a mind reader!"

"It's not so simple, Zara!" you tell her. "I'm still training, you know. And even if I were a master, it's not an exact science."

You focus harder. "He's not supposed to be here," you say. "He didn't want to come. The older man made him. He wants to go home."

"Okay, not bad," Zara says, nodding.

You furrow your brow and try to concentrate. "His name. Is Arjun."

Zara makes a big show of clapping and bows her head to you. "Now that is useful information."

You withdraw from Arjun's mind, exhausted by the effort. You were so focused on reading the boy that you didn't notice everyone else had finished eating.

"Oh, we better get a move on!" exclaims Saeed, jumping up. "We have to get to post-meal chore section!"

You start to rise, but a firm hand lands on your shoulder. You look up. It's Chandh Sahib, and Dev Acharya is standing just behind him. *Uh-oh.*

"Hunting for information?" Chandh Sahib asks in a deceptively mild tone.

"Uh, gotta go!" says Zara, jumping up. "See ya, Krishi!" she calls over her shoulder, gesturing for Saeed to run along with her.

You gulp.

"Since by now you know my charge's name," says Dev Acharya severely, "I will ask you to look out for him. He is a new student here at the Citadel."

He's a little old, you think to yourself, *to* begin *training*. He looks about the same age as you and your friends, and you've already been here four years.

"Yes," says Dev, as if you had spoken out loud, "he is older than the normal beginning student. His parents are merchants and are often at sea. We missed the opportunity to collect him several times. But he has the skill and affinity for the arts we practice. And so he has come to be here. You are responsible for him now," he says to you, looking directly into your eyes. You feel something shift as he says it, and somehow you know that you will look out for Arjun, no matter what happens.

What just happened? Did Dev Acharya cast some kind of charm on you?

"Events move quickly, Krishi," says Chandh Sahib then. "You have proven tonight that you can be trusted with greater responsibility." He pauses. "Though one hopes you will learn not to be caught when you are reading another."

You flush darkly.

"Meet us in three hours in the observation salon. There are decisions to make." And with that mysterious pronouncement, he and Dev Acharya withdraw. You look for Arjun, but the boy is nowhere to be seen. You briefly consider casting out with your mind to find him, but think better of it, considering your earlier indiscretion.

You retreat to your room and try to study, but you can barely concentrate. After a dead boring assignment on Narbolin court poetry—endless epics filled with combat and conquests—followed by an attempt to practice one of the peculiar stringed instruments of the Cyrene lowlands, you complete a brief assignment on the wild martial dance of the ancient and forgotten Yevadi warriors of the far north.

As soon as you dare, you close up your books and head out, taking the stairs two at a time up the western stairwell to the observation salon. It sits at the top of the Citadel, just below the ramparts. Its great curved window gives the widest possible view of the horizon looking north toward Elaria. The ceiling in the observation salon is also a great sheet of refracted glass, allowing one to observe the stars and the moons.

You skid to a halt in front of the great oaken doors, one of which is slightly ajar. Beyond, in the darkening room, the fire has been lit and you hear someone singing an odd yet familiar tune.

"And when the moons rise / send me out to sea / my heart grows like the moonlight flows / and serene forever I shall be . . ."

You walk in quietly, trying not to disturb the singer. It is the sea captain you saw earlier. She sits near the fire on a stool, a long pipe in her hand. She fills it with dried green leaves she takes from a pouch at her belt.

"It's a Kulsumi song," you say to her, remembering where you'd heard it.

She looks at you with a sardonic smile and gestures with a little bow. "As I am Kulsumi, it's a Kulsumi song I should sing."

"I thought it was unusual for women to be captaining and sailing," you say.

"I am an unusual woman," she says simply, lighting her pipe and puffing away. "Dalilah Kulsum, at your service."

The doors open again, this time with a crash. Chandh Sahib enters, followed by Dev Acharya, Sandhya, Zara, Saeed, some of the other senior students, and, to your surprise, Arjun.

"Time rises up," Chandh Sahib says as the sky outside darkens. "You three students," he murmurs, "are special here at the Citadel. You are different from each other, and different

15

from the Whisperers who came before you. You did not know it this morning, but your Time has come early." He scans over you, Zara, Saeed, and Arjun. You feel his eyes return to you. What does he mean? And why is *Arjun* here?

"I too wish there was more time for you all to train. I wish even more so that you could take the Tests for which you have been preparing, but Time itself has decided to move on ahead of us. We must act quickly to catch up."

He gestures to the chairs, arranged in a loose oval in the center of the chamber. Dev and Sandhya sit, and he turns, with his back to the view of the sea through the panoramic window, to address everyone. You and the other students stand, waiting. The Captain remains by the fire, smoking her pipe, watching the small assembly through squinted eyes.

"Last month the Emperor of Narbolis sent a Writ of Accession to the King of Albahr."

"A Writ of Accession?" you ask.

"It is a document by which Albahr would voluntarily join the Narbolin Empire. In the Emperor's eyes it's probably akin to a peace agreement. It also not-so-subtly announces his intention to invade militarily if the Writ is not signed."

"Why does the Emperor want Albahr?" you ask. "It's on the other side of the continent from his capital."

"We can only assume he plans to take all eastern Elaria eventually. Faldorn may be closer, but the mountains lie between the Emperor and that city. And Sky Home is well protected in the Northern Range," explains Dev Acharya.

"Besides," the boy Arjun interrupts, "Albahr controls all the shipping lanes on this side of the continent. The Emperor wouldn't *need* the other kings to obey if he controlled Albahr."

"The society of Narbolis has been acquiring land and kingdoms and territories for a hundred years. Their emperors and empresses have been singular in this desire for generations," adds Chandh Sahib sadly.

"But what's the problem?" Zara asks. "If the King refuses, there's not much the Emperor can do, is there? The mountains lie between us and him. Or if he comes by sea, then the Duchy of Kulsum will stop him."

"Well, issuance of the Writ is our immediate problem," says Chandh Sahib. "The Emperor has taken the somewhat unusual step of expelling all the Whisperers from his court. Without their presence, we have no idea what he's planning, but we know he's planning something. Something big."

"What is the King going to do?" you ask.

Dev coughs lightly. "That is our second problem," he says. "The King has vanished. No one is sure where he went. It is possible the Narbolins have him, and it is also possible that he escaped on his own. But no one knows where he is or what happened. The situation is—delicate. The governing council has detained all the Whisperers in the capital, and those remaining in outer Narbolis are many days' journey away. I'm afraid that Chandh Shahib and the Whisperers here in the Citadel must return with me now."

"How far a sea journey is it?" you ask out loud. Everyone turns toward you, curiosity piqued by the peculiar question. Sea travel is so unusual, even for the very brave.

"I can get you there by daybreak if we leave quickly," the Captain says then.

"Impossible!" Sandhya snaps.

"I know the secret water-roads," the Captain says simply.

"No one knows all of them," Sandhya says. "Only the Duke himself could travel that quickly and be in possession of those maps!"

She shrugs diffidently.

"The Duke," you say, realization slowly dawning, "or the Duchess."

The Captain twirls her hand and bows once more in that sardonic way. "Dalilah, the Duchess of Kulsum, at your service."

"How is it the Duchess has permission from her husband to captain a war galleon?" Zara asks.

The Duchess smiles. "She doesn't."

"Captain a war galleon?" Zara asks.

"Have his permission," the Duchess answers.

"The Duchess can be trusted," Dev interrupts. "If she says she can get us there by daybreak, she can."

"We must learn what is happening," Chandh Sahib says. "If you permit me, I will look abroad on the sea." He turns to face the wide window. You edge closer to him. You have never seen this kind of reaching out. Chandh Sahib's eyes lose focus and somehow you can sense his awareness stretching out, through the window and over the sea.

"What is he doing?" You hear Saeed's voice in your ear.

You cast out in your mind toward Saeed, willing him to hear you. *He's looking out over the ocean*, you think. *He's trying to see if the water is clear.* You cast a quick glance over to Saeed, and by his wide eyes you can tell he heard you.

"That settles it," Chandh Sahib says then, turning away from the window and back toward you. "There's a fleet out there, heading this way and flying Narbolin flags. If we leave quickly, we can evade them before they blockade the Citadel." He glances toward the Duchess for confirmation and she gives him a curt nod. He turns back to the rest of you. "But the Citadel also must be defended. I do not know the intentions of this fleet. Under no circumstances can the Narbolins be allowed to land here while I am gone. There is too great a risk that they will try to claim its secrets."

Dev turns toward you and your friends. "Zara and Saeed, I must request that you join Chandh Sahib and me, leaving for Albahr tonight. If it is true that the King is no longer in the city, there will be a power vacuum, and the Narbolins must not be allowed to seize control of the ruling council."

"Sandhya will remain here at the Citadel," Chandh Sahib says.

"Arjun must stay here also," Dev declares. "It is not safe for him to return. His father is on the council."

"Krishi," says Chandh Sahib. "You would be an excellent help on the ground in Albahr, and yet the Citadel must be protected. Where do you feel you can do the most good?"

You look from Chandh Sahib's eyes over to your friends. You want to go with them. The thought of them alone, in danger, without you, makes your stomach hurt. And yet you remember your mysterious exchange with Dev in the dining hall. You made a promise to him, to help protect Arjun.

"Krishi, you have a fateful decision before you. We know

the Citadel must be protected. But you cannot grow further here. The time has come to test your skills of magic and combat on the Continent."

You look toward Dev. "Is this a test?"

"Every moment is a test, Krishi," says Chandh Sahib gently. "Every choice you make defines your destiny from that point."

If you decide to stay at the Citadel with Sandhya and Arjun and see to its defense, go to section 2.

If you decide to join Zara and Saeed and go to the mainland with Chandh Sahib, go to section 36.

SECTION 2

"**I** think I should stay here," you say. Chandh Sahib smiles, taking your hand in both of his.

"Yes. You must stay. Protect the Citadel." He leans closer and speaks in a lower tone, so only you can hear. "Look after Arjun. He is a new student and doesn't know very much about our ways." He turns to the others. "It's time," he says crisply, clapping his hands. "We must leave at once."

The Duchess rises, her earlier languor evaporated. "I shall prepare the ship. My crew will be ready as soon as you are, my lords. I have a small escort myself, two other ships patrolling. They'll sound the alarm if the Narbolins get too close." She departs, winking at you.

"Everyone else, prepare to depart within the half hour," Dev orders, and the group disperses.

You start to follow Zara and Saeed, hoping for a chance to say goodbye, but Chandh Sahib puts his hand on your arm, holding you back as the room empties. "You saw what I did?" he asks you, gesturing toward the window.

You nod. "You went out on the water with your mind."

"You can find me if you need me, Krishi. Listen, behta." He pauses. "There are secrets on the island. Weapons if you need them. Defense. But there are things that cannot be taught or told. They must be learned."

Now what does that mean?

You had your reasons for remaining behind, but you have a hard time knowing that Saeed and Zara are about to embark on a great adventure. You go down the staircase to the docks and find the little party huddled at the pier, waiting to board the Duchess's ship.

Zara and Saeed stand together, traveling cloaks covering the nondescript tunics and leggings they wear. Saeed's mop of curls is hidden beneath a woolen cap, and Zara has pulled the deep cowl of her tunic over her head.

"Welcome aboard the *Blade*, travelers!" calls out the Duchess from the ship rail.

"It's time," says Chandh Sahib.

"Don't get captured!" you call after your friends as they walk up the gangplank.

You and Arjun are left standing alone on the dock as the sailors cast off and the galleon makes its way out into the harbor.

"I suppose I'm stuck with you," Arjun says in a flat tone, casting a critical eye at you.

"Don't be too excited about it," you retort, but he's already spun on his heel and begun heading back to the staircase.

You follow him, pausing at the tapestry. You look up at the fire being flung down onto the ramparts by the Whisperers. You remember Chandh Sahib's words. There was something he wasn't telling you—or *couldn't* tell you. You sigh and follow Arjun up the stairs. If morning brings a blockade, you had best get some sleep tonight.

Your sleep is fitful because you worry about your friends all night. At daybreak, the sun filters into your room and you rise, throwing a cloak around your body as you climb up the ramparts and look out over the sparkling sea. The sun is so bright on the water, you find it hard to see. There is a spyglass mounted, but as you swing it across the horizon, you can't spot any ships.

"You're going to have to know where to look," says someone behind you. You turn toward the staircase coming up to the ramparts from the observation salon, and there stands Arjun. "You won't be able to pick them out against the open sea. It's like trying to find one single star in the night sky. You have to know where to point your spyglass."

"How is THAT supposed to help me?" you say sourly. Arjun's act is getting old.

He shrugs. "Isn't there anything around here that can help you look? I thought there were all kinds of magical weapons lying around," he says.

"Magic objects can't be used by students at the Citadel," you say impatiently. "I don't know where they stash them, but it isn't here. You're not even supposed to use magic, except in extreme circumstances." When you look over, you realize Arjun's jaw is clenching and unclenching. Is he scared?. You soften your tone a bit. "Though I'd say this *is* pretty extreme. We have to find out if Chandh Sahib and the others made it past the blockade. And it would help to know what to expect from those ships, too."

"Try that spell your teacher did," Arjun suggests.

"I don't think I'm strong enough. We're too far from the open sea. There's a breakwater that protects the harbor. But there *is* a promontory that sticks out from the cliffs at the far end of the harbor. If we climbed up there I'd have a better chance at reaching out over open sea."

You remember the images from the tapestry—Whisperers on the ramparts flinging fire down toward the ships. They had to be casting some kind of spell, you realize, though it's not one you ever learned.

Go to section 3.

SECTION 3

"We have to find out whether Chandh Sahib and the others made it past those ships. There's no time to go inland."

Arjun pauses for a moment, and then nods. "It's your call, Krishi," he says, and you feel grateful for his support, forgetting your earlier annoyance with him.

Sandhya is busy marshaling the remaining students in the Citadel's defense, so it is easy for you to slip out into the courtyard and through the side door that leads to the trails along the rocky coast.

As you climb, the strong winds from the sea hit you. The salt in the air energizes you and you press on. The trail is a steep one. After a while, you only know Arjun is still with you by the sound of his heavy breath behind you.

The trail ends at a vista over the open sea. Down to your left is the deep harbor with access to the Citadel's docking cave. On your right the trail continues down into the wooded interior of the island.

"Okay," says Arjun. "How do you do it?"

You turn away from him, somewhat guilty that you reached out into his mind at the dinner. "Well, you know how sometimes you are in a crowded room and you try to listen for just one person's voice?"

He smiles. "Yes, I've been at a lot of those kinds of dinners and . . ." he suddenly catches himself and stops abruptly. "I'm sorry, what were you saying?"

"It's like that, except you are reaching out to listen with something more than your ear—it's like you are trying to listen with your mind. Someone like me learns how to hear sounds and language first, but if you're really good you can actually SEE things, or smell things."

"So . . . you could hear what people are thinking?" he asks, with a little smile. "What am I thinking right now?" Arjun fixes you with his kohl-rimmed eyes, that one lock of glossy black hair falling out of his ponytail onto his cheek.

You turn from him, flushing. "It's not polite to read someone's thoughts unless you are on a mission."

"But I'm asking you to," he says, still smiling.

Good thing you don't know what I'm thinking right now, you think to yourself, and turn back to the sea.

"Maybe later," you say. "Let's focus on the task at hand."

"Got it, master Krishi," he says, teasing you. "What do you need me to do?"

"Well," you say, thinking about how to put it. "You know how when someone is trying to climb a tree and you get under them and you don't exactly PUSH them up but you kind of support them?"

"So they don't fall?" Arjun asks dubiously. Whatever he did

in his previous life, you are fairly certain it didn't involve climbing trees.

"Yes." You smile at him. "So I want you to try to do that with your mind. Don't direct it out at the sea, just think toward me, thoughts of support and comfort. Like you have my back."

"I have your back," Arjun says simply, putting one hand right below your shoulder blades. "Is this okay?" he asks then, aware he hadn't asked you.

"Yes, it's actually good. Your hand on my back will remind me you're supporting me and it will remind you to stay steady with it."

"I guess the masters don't need tricks like this."

You smile and turn your focus out to the sea. Slowly, with an awareness of both Arjun's hand on your back and his mind behind you holding you up, you reach out in wide arcs, trying to feel for Chandh Sahib's presence. There's nothing.

"I can't feel him," you say calmly, trying not to think the worst.

"Maybe he is shielding?" Arjun suggests. "What about Saeed or Zara? Can you feel them?"

You change your intention and somehow, distantly, you feel a twin spark, a flicker like fireflies in the night.

"They're through," you say exhaling in relief. "They ran the blockade. They're halfway to Albahr."

"Find the Narbolins," Arjun urges, his voice sounding like it's coming from a great distance. You swing away from the pricks of sensation that marked Saeed and Zara's presences and range again across the ocean. The ships are nowhere to be found. Have they fled?

"I'm pulling back," you say to Arjun and begin drawing yourself back to your body, like reeling in a long line. As you soar mentally back to the island, back to the promontory, it's as if you stumble on a stone on the floor. You start to develop an awareness only a few leagues out from the island. "It's the Narbolin ships! They've been traveling the water-roads too! They didn't even try to stop the Duchess because they're on their way here!"

"Whoa!" Arjun steps back from you and you both shake out your limbs. They feel prickly and frozen the way they feel when you sit for too long.

"They had ground troops with them, Arjun! They were close enough to the island that I could see them."

"I don't understand," he says with alarm. "How would they dare to storm the Citadel? It's protected by the treaty of the Inviolate!"

"I don't know," you say. "It's clear that the Narbolins don't want the Whisperers to get involved in whatever is happening in the capital."

"What do we do?" Arjun asks calmly, all business. "Can you do some magic and wreck the ships?"

"I'm not that strong," you say. You snap your fingers. "The beacon on the ramparts! We can light the beacon and Chandh Sahib and the others might see it."

"There's a storm coming in," Arjun observes, pointing to a gray smudge on the western horizon.

A storm . . .

"The Heart of the Storm," you say. Arjun's eyes ask a silent question. "It's an ancient monolith at the center of the island.

There's a pathway that leads straight to it. The Whisperers can draw from its energy, even at the Citadel. I've never learned how to draw from it, but maybe if I could actually put my hands on the rock I could . . ."

"You could what?" Arjun asks impatiently. "If you haven't noticed, there's an armada bearing down on us. It's about to get crowded on this island!"

Your eyes fix on the smudge of storm in the distance. "Maybe I could call the storm in."

"Even IF you can figure out how to work the magic, we will really have to hurry, Krishi. Do you think there's time?"

If you want to try to use the Heart of the Storm to draw the storm in and shield the harbor, go to section 5.

If you think you should return to the Citadel instead and light the beacon, go to section 6.

SECTION 4

"All this sneaking around at night isn't going to do us any good if someone can just as easily sneak up behind us," you say. "Besides, who would be docking in the dead of the night? If those are the smugglers we'll kill two birds with one stone."

"Stroke two cats with one hand," Etheldreda corrects you, absently.

"What now?" Saeed asks.

"Stroke two cats," she repeats. "Why are we always killing animals?"

You stare at her blankly.

"When my maedaw ran this place, we raised vegetables and grain only. We had animals for labor and for the milk and eggs but we didn't kill them, and we definitely didn't eat them."

"So what then," Saeed says, "after they stopped giving milk you would just keep them? In an old folks' paddock?"

Etheldreda's lips pucker. "Yes," she snaps. "What else are you supposed to do with your old workers? Kill and eat them?"

"As interesting as this philosophical debate is," you interrupt urgently, "I think it's time to make a move. Saeed, you take Etheldreda toward the office and see what you can find. I'm going to investigate the docking cave."

As they steal off toward the kitchen, you cautiously enter the darkened staircase. After one flight down, the angular staircase enters the bare rock of the cliff the house is built on. From that point on, it turns into a spiral staircase, though it is cut wide, likely to accommodate freight being brought up from below. The only light in the staircase is from the kitchen torches above and the torches that are lit in the cavern below, so it is easy for you to proceed downward in the dark.

"All right, boys! That wasn't bad sailing," says one of the voices in the cavern below.

"I wouldn't put in for your captain's ribbon yet," declares another voice imperiously.

Now where have you heard that voice before? You pause in the dark.

You hear the sound of a muffled struggle and then the sound of someone being smacked sharply.

"That'll do," the first voice says with menace.

Something's not right, you think. If these are smugglers, why are they bringing in a prisoner? A prisoner with a voice you think you recognize, but cannot place. The shadows are deep enough that you feel you could sneak all the way down into the cavern, but then you would have to handle whatever you found on your own.

If you steal back upstairs to try to catch up with Saeed and Etheldreda, go to section 15.

If you sneak down the rest of the way, go to section 16.

SECTION 5

"*E*ven if we get the beacon lit, there's no way of knowing if Chandh Sahib and the others will even see it," you say decisively. "And if they see it, that doesn't mean they are going to make it back to help us."

"Yes," Arjun agrees. "They might even get in more trouble trying to help us." He looks afraid.

"It's up to us," you say, putting your hand on his shoulder to reassure him. "We can do this, Arjun."

He bites his lip, still unsure.

"Listen," you say, knowing that you are going to need his support again, no matter what spell you try at the Heart of the Storm. "I know you just got here to the Citadel and all of this is new, but we aren't inventing anything. We are just reaching inside of ourselves and reaching back out into the world around us, trying to realize the connections that have always been there. Chandh Sahib taught us that the storm, that storm out over the ocean, it's already inside us. We can draw it out—or draw it in."

Arjun looks at you and smiles, the first smile you've seen him make. "How did you get so brave, Krishi?"

"Brave?" you ask, surprised. "Me? I'm afraid of everything."

"But you aren't," he says, shaking his head. "You're willing to do anything to protect people. I want to be that brave."

"You're being brave now. You're helping me protect the Citadel."

"I don't feel brave," says Arjun. "I feel scared."

"Bravery isn't what you feel, Arjun," you say, faking confidence you don't really feel. "It's what you do."

You backtrack along the ridge to the fork in the path. One branch leads down into the dark leafy interior forest and the other continues up into the rocky crags in the center of the island. You take that branch. The trees get sparser as you climb. You catch glimpses of the sapphire sea between the trunks. Then, just past a sweetly jangling waterfall, the pool beneath it swirling with dark currents, you reach the clearing in which lies the enormous boulder that is the Heart of the Storm.

Arjun whistles in awe. "It must be fifty feet long!"

You walk up to the massive boulder, rumored to be one of the most ancient stones on the entire planet. It is one of the original boulders that pressed up from beneath the earth when Elaria rose from the sea in long-forgotten eons. The great stone is riven with deep blue veins of some kind of crystal, and the whole rock speckles silver in the light. In one great blue crevasse two thirds of the way down the rock, previous visitors have left offerings of small stones and flowers. A few half-burned candles are collected at the opening.

"I'm going to try to call the storm in," you say over your shoulder. "It's far out, so I don't know how this will go. Hopefully at least I can pull some rain and fog to disguise the breakwater and the harbor. With any luck the invaders won't be able to find the Citadel."

"Do you need help?" Arjun asks.

"I'm not sure what power lies within the stone. Let me try alone first and see what happens." You don't express your worry that Arjun—and you—might be overcome by the ancient magic surging within the stone.

You turn from him to face the stone and place your palms against the cool granite. In your mind you visualize the storm. You can zoom in on the water and air of it instinctively. You press your fingertips down and lift your palms up off the stone, feeling cool air flow between your skin and the stone. With the water and air in your mind, you gently try to draw energy up from the stone to summon in the fog and rain.

As soon as you focus your energy on the stone you feel a potent swell of power, and immediately the wind rushes in. You hear thunder and lightning at the shore. "What happened?" you say, in shock. You spin around to face Arjun, who is cheering.

"You did it! You did it!" he cries, jumping up and down and clapping you on the back.

"But how? I hardly got a chance to try! I just thought of it and it happened in a surge."

"It's the stone," guesses Arjun. "It must be that powerful." He pauses then, his eyes narrowing. "Krishi, if it was that easy to pull in rain and fog, you could probably pull in the entire typhoon and destroy the fleet."

That power that flowed from the Heart of the Storm felt immense. You feel confident that you could pull in the typhoon. But is it the right thing to do? Chandh Sahib warned you that magic was only meant for the most extreme circumstances. On the other hand, what is more extreme than the Narbolins taking over the Citadel? Imagine what would happen if they gained access to the stone!

"You can handle it, Krishi, I know you can." Arjun puts his hand on your shoulder and smiles at you. "I believe in you."

You pause. Arjun's words warm you in the cooling winds that are now blowing through the trees from the storm. Still, the stone is clearly an artifact of great power. Maybe you should explore it a little more.

If you decide to pull in the full typhoon in order to destroy the invading fleet, go to section 7.

If you think it wiser to take the time to examine the stone, go to section 8.

SECTION 6

"It's too risky to try to move the storm," you say to Arjun. "I don't know enough magic to channel a storm. Too much could go wrong. Besides, that storm is heading this way. It will get here eventually, without any help from me."

"So it's back to the Citadel to sound the alarm," Arjun says decisively.

You turn back from the outcropping and begin running toward the Citadel. Arjun is running behind you, but you can tell that he is not used to this level of exertion. You turn back and reach out for his hand.

"Come on!" you cry out.

Arjun lets you pull him along, and the two of you race back to the Citadel as fast as you can. You reach the courtyard, where everything is quiet.

You run up the half flight of stairs to the main kitchen, where you hear the clang of pots and pans as the cooks prepare for the midday meal.

"Nobody knows what's happening," says Arjun, panting and out of breath.

Think, Krishi, think! you say to yourself. Suraj would be with the younger students in the Great Hall for dance class. That's the closest classroom, and the youngest students are the most vulnerable. But Sandhya is the combat teacher. She'd be the most help in this situation, but she's not teaching right now and you have no idea where to find her. If your earlier attempt to locate Chandh Sahib telepathically was any indication, you doubt you will be able to read Sandhya's presence in the Citadel.

If you think it's better to go to the Great Hall and find Suraj, go to section 93.

If you head upstairs to the masters' offices to look for Sandhya, go to section 94.

SECTION 7

"We have to take the chance," you decide. "If the Narbolins land, the Citadel does not have enough Whisperers to fend them off."

You turn back to the stone. The last time felt easy, so you're sure you can manage it without Arjun's help. In fact, you would feel better if he stayed at a safe distance. You glance over your shoulder. He stands just a little bit off, looking at you with concern, plucking the hem of his garment. He gives you a weak smile.

You turn back to the stone and place your palms flat against it. You bow your head down and brace yourself. Traveling now through the rain you've already called in, you reach out for the full power of the storm that rages out at sea.

As soon as you feel the crackle and heat of the lightning high in the air, you roar and drag it down toward the Citadel. A great rush of energy passes through you. The typhoon is coming at full speed. The wind whips and lashes at you, and Arjun screams.

Arjun grabs you from behind. He pulls a fistful of your tunic in one hand, throwing his other arm around your chest to pull you back. You fall all the way backward onto the ground, heaving with exertion. The rain pours down in torrents around you.

"What happened?" you shout over the roaring storm.

"You were circled in fire! I pulled at you but it was almost like you were fused to the rock."

You prop yourself up on your elbows and wipe the water out of your face. "You saved me," you say simply.

He stares into your eyes for a moment. He seems about to say something and then there is a bolt of lightning above you.

"We have to get out of the forest!" he yells.

Sandhya is going to kill us, you think. You grab Arjun's hand and the two of you run from the clearing and down the mountain trail back to the ramparts, careful on the slick stones.

Even though it is midmorning, the storm has covered the sky so completely it seems like twilight. Through the curtains of rain you see the students gathered together on the rampart, huddled beneath the awning that protects the beacon. There's no hope of lighting it now. You spot Sandhya.

Go to section 22.

SECTION 8

"No, Arjun," you say. "The stone is too powerful and we don't know enough about it."

"So then let's find out more about it," he says, grabbing your hand.

"Why is this so important to you?" you ask him, noticing how agitated he seems.

He rubs his face and pushes his hair back in the now-drizzling rain. "I'm sorry. I just want to do something. It's so frustrating being sent out here and not being able to help . . . the King."

"Do you know him?" you ask.

"Me? Know the King?" he says quickly. "No. Of course not. But—we're his people. I want to help him."

Odd. For someone who is about to undergo training as a Whisperer, you'd think Arjun would be a better liar. He *does* know the King, that much is obvious. But if he's spending any amount of time with Dev Acharya, that would only make sense. What's clear is that Arjun wants to drop it, so you drop it.

"Well," you say, "the rain is only going to get worse. I think we should get back to the Citadel, but let's at least check out the stone before we go. I've never been up this far."

The two of you circle the massive rock. A rounder face of the stone extends to the edge of the clearing. As you walk along its length you see the sides become craggier and more vertical, and at the far end it seems to be embedded in the side of the ridge. As you get closer to the brilliant blue crevasse in the side, you hear Arjun take a sharp breath.

It's not just a crevasse. It seems to lead *into* the stone.

"A portal?" Arjun asks.

"One way to find out," you say, and cautiously enter the darkness. There are shallow steps and you feel yourself lean forward slowly in the pitch black. From somewhere up ahead you see a deep green light shining.

As you approach, the light fills more space, but it is still very dim. "Is it magic?" Arjun asks.

"Phosphorescent stones, more likely," you say. "Magic comes out of people. Rocks and trees can *store* magical energy—like the Heart of the Storm—but it has to be channeled by a person; they don't usually manifest it on their own."

"Unless there's someone in here," hisses Arjun.

For a wild moment you look around for a weapon you could grab hold of, but slowly you realize it isn't logical. Who would be living here? Beneath the stone?

The narrow hallway you have been following ends in a chamber almost twenty feet across. You are in the heart of the Heart of the Storm now, but just like a storm from nature, there is a calm here.

Before you is a loose semicircle of three plinths, rising up from the rock floor. On each pedestal there is a small boat. They are narrow and old-fashioned, identical except in their colors: one glows silver, another golden, and the third glows a deep blue. It's the combination of the lights that seemed green in the long hallway.

"I thought you said objects don't manifest magical properties without a human channeling the power," Arjun says.

"They don't," you say, approaching the three boats with wonder. "I don't know what these are." As you get close, you notice myriad long sea-oars protruding from the sides. These are ancient boats, very unlike the ones that sail the seas now.

"They're barques," says Arjun from behind you. "The kind that would bear the body of the king and his attendants into the afterlife. There was always a solar barque and a lunar barque," he says, gesturing to the boat glowing silver and the other glowing golden.

"Then what's this one?" you wonder, approaching the third bluish-glowing barque. It's speckled inside with numerous pricks of light. "The starry barque?"

"Whoa, Krishi, look at this!" Arjun exclaims from the plinth bearing the solar barque. He stands on tiptoe and peers down into the boat. You hurry over and look with him. There in the depths you see an image of the ramparts above the Citadel. The great beacon is unlit. The blue sea shows beyond. Is it a painting? A vision? Then you see a great albatross flying in from the sea. It lands on the rocks and folds its wings.

"Wait," you say, and rush to the lunar barque. You look down into its depths. You see the docks, the water, the sailing boats. Dockworkers are scurrying about, securing the boats and pulling the great chain across the harbor.

"The barques are scrying devices, I think," you say. "Portholes to another place."

"In the old stories," Arjun says, "the barques could carry you across the night sky."

You go back to peer into the starry barque. There's nothing there but the deep night sky. You keep looking, captivated, certain there is some great power within, if only you could interpret it.

"Can we use the barques to change what's happening in the places they show us?" you wonder.

"We've already called in the storm," Arjun says. "Maybe it would be worth lighting the beacon as well."

"I'm not sure," you say. The dockworkers looked like they could use some help pulling that chain across. If you can get it locked in, the larger Narbolin boats will not be able to approach the Citadel.

On the other hand, something of great power lurks in the starry barque. You did not sense danger there, only great potential. The most basic technique of channeling energy from an object is to place one's hands on it. You feel the power of the barques now that you have been in the room longer.

If you use the lunar barque, go to section 9.

If you use the starry barque, go to section 81.

If you use the solar barque, go to section 102.

SECTION 9

"We need to help the dockworkers!" you say. "With this rain, no one will even see the beacon."

You and Arjun approach the lunar barque from opposite sides and you each place your hands on its hull, your fingertips almost touching. You look down into the hull of the barque and see the docks again. You imagine yourself there. You have the sensation of being immersed in water. You reach out for Arjun but you can't feel anything. There is a great swell beneath you as if you are being borne up by a current or a wave. Everything is dark around you and you instinctively hold your breath.

There is a light up ahead and you begin swimming—through what? air? water? smoke?—toward it. It gets brighter and brighter and before you know it, you and Arjun spill out onto the ground before the tapestry in the docks. No one seems to have noticed you. You look back toward the tapestry. It looks the same as it always did. You brush your hands against it. It's solid.

"Come on," you say to Arjun and run toward the crews, who are cranking the great gears on either side of the mouth of the cave that will pull the massive chain up out of the water and taut against the mouth of the cave. Without even checking to see if he's followed you, you join the other students, pulling and yanking at the gear-wheel with all your might. There is a massive groaning sound as the chain starts reeling in as it rises out of the sea.

"Keep pulling," you shout, even while twisting around to try to catch a glimpse of Arjun. He's nowhere to be seen. Figures. It takes a lot of energy and a lot of sweat, but you manage to drag the chain across the harbor. As you and the others fall back, panting from your exertions, Sandhya's voice rings out in the cavern.

"Students!" she calls. "Those who can fight, report to the ramparts! Those who are not prepared, meet Suraj in the Great Hall!"

"Krishi!" You hear someone closer calling your name. It's Arjun! "Krishi, I'm going to the Great Hall. I don't know how to fight, I'm not ready!"

Go to section 11.

SECTION 10

*A*rjun steps out beside you, and together you climb the staircase up from the ramparts. It's made of hundreds of steps set directly into the rock wall. Wind from the sea blows at you as you climb and climb. You finally reach the beacon at the crest of the craggy mountain that the Citadel is built into.

The beacon itself is a neatly stacked quadrangle of fuel-coated logs. There is a vented canopy over it to allow the smoke to escape while still protecting it from the elements. In the years that you have lived in the Citadel, you have never seen it lit, but you know it is used as a night warning during storms and as an emergency beacon during the day.

The normal flame of the wood is enhanced by whatever compound the Whisperers coated the wood with, and whatever witchery they mustered into the wood itself.

As you've been told, the beacon shines so brightly, even in the daytime, that it can be seen for leagues in any direction, including, some say—if one knows where to look for it—all the way to Albahr. Yet by some enchantment, it cannot be seen from the Citadel itself so that its use remains sequestered from the students and they are protected from news of whatever emergency the beacon calls out in.

Far below you, on the ramparts, you see the students and Sandhya streaming out from the lower levels on the parapets. They are preparing the Citadel's defense.

"Let's do it," you say to Arjun. You approach the mechanism at rock face. It is fixed into one of four pillars that stand at sentinel around the beacon, supporting the canopy. The gear and crank activate a huge rock-flint at the base of the beacon to ignite it.

Arjun stands back on the staircase while you crank the gear. You hear the sound of stone grinding against stone, and then with a great *WHUFF* the beacon blazes aflame.

Instinctually you throw up your hand to protect your face from the heat, but a split second later, you realize there is no heat coming from the blazing beacon. Stranger and stranger.

"Come on!" Arjun shouts, pointing. You look out to sea in the direction he is gesturing and see four ships approaching the cliffs of the Citadel. It's happening.

You race down the stairs toward the ramparts.

Go to section 12.

SECTION 11

You and Arjun run up the staircase and down the corridor into the Great Hall. A crowd of younger students has gathered there around Suraj. He looks over at you.

"Krishi, Arjun! The moons shine on us! Sandhya and the senior students are up on the ramparts. We don't have much time. Since these students can't fight, we've got to take refuge somewhere in the Citadel." You can tell that Suraj is working hard to keep his voice calm as he looks around the sea of frightened faces and smiles widely. "Now, I know you scamps know where the best hiding places in the Citadel are."

One of the younger students, Dimple, raises her hand timidly. "We hide in the root cellar beneath the kitchens sometimes."

Suraj smiles. "That would be the safest, and it's the closest to where we are now." He catches you frowning. "Krishi, what is it?"

"I think I have an idea, Suraj. If you trust me."

For a long moment Suraj looks at you, hesitating. Then Arjun steps up beside you and puts his hand on your shoulder. "I trust Krishi."

Suraj's expression changes, and he tilts his head, regarding Arjun quizzically. "Very well," he says. "Lead us, Krishi."

You hesitate. Your thought is to bring them to the cavern by the docks. The Narbolins will be so focused on securing the Citadel that they won't backtrack to the docks, will they? The kitchens are closer though, and you can already hear the clash of steel in the floors below. Somehow the soldiers have gotten through, or else they landed somewhere else and scaled the cliffs.

If you lead the students down to the cavern at the docks, go to section 13.

If you lead the students to the kitchens like Suraj suggested, go to section 82.

SECTION 12

$\int$ andhya is huddled up with the senior students before the crenelated battlement, issuing orders.

"Sandhya!" you call out, and she looks up in surprise.

You and Arjun skid to a halt in front of her.

"The Narbolins are coming!" Arjun says, breathlessly.

Sandhya is grim.

"The Narbolins are here," she says, gesturing out to the harbor. A row of ships blockades the exit from the docking cave. Several smaller ships bristle with pike-bearing soldiers who row for the docks.

"So it's happened," Arjun says grimly, his mouth settling into an unpleasant frown you are not sure the meaning of.

"Krishi, tell me exactly what you did so I know which defense measures to activate."

If you say, "We called in a storm and lit the beacon," go to section 21.

If you say you only lit the beacon, go to section 23.

SECTION 13

"Follow me!" you say, and Suraj creeps over to the great double doors leading out into the main hallway. He puts his ear to the crack and then looks back at you, shaking his head.

"The side doors in the wings of the stage," you say quickly, and Suraj nods his agreement, gesturing you onward.

You run for the far end of the Great Hall, Arjun alongside you and the young students just behind. Arjun holds Dimple's hand and helps her keep up. *She looks scared*, you think.

You reach the small stage and mount the short flight of steps. You wave the students on to the wings and over to the small door. You look back. Suraj is still at the main doors listening.

"Suraj," you mouth silently at him. When he speaks, you hear his voice in your ear as if he is next to you.

"Go, Krishi. Keep them safe. I'll catch up."

You don't hesitate. You hear Suraj fling the doors open, yelping like a wildcat to draw the attention of whoever is in the hallways.

Soldiers in the Citadel. You never thought you would see the day. You and the young students creep down the side hallway and up the main corridor. Just across it is the twisting stairway that leads down to the docking cavern. You hear the sounds of fighting in the hallway.

"It's now or never," you say to Arjun. "You run straight across the hallway with the kids." You turn to the younger students. "You guys run and keep running. You follow Arjun, okay? No one stays back."

"What about you?" Arjun asks, with concern in his eyes. "Krishi, you're coming with us, right? We need you."

"I'll be right behind you," you reassure him. "I just need to check on Suraj first and run interference in case anyone sees us. Okay," you say. "It's go time."

And with that, Arjun, still holding Dimple's hand, rushes across the main corridor, the other students following. You run alongside them and pause, looking up the main corridor to Suraj. He is crouched low in a fighting stance. Four Narbolin soldiers, all armed with swords, surround him.

If you stick with the plan and follow Arjun and the others down the staircase, go to section 83.

If you think Suraj is in too much danger, and intervene, go to section 84.

SECTION 14

"Quick," you say, scrambling for the far end of the kitchen. "You're sure the office is this way?"

"It's been there for years," affirms Etheldreda.

You duck through the door into the darkened dining room. The long table is set for breakfast. Along your right is a wide window that runs the length of the room and looks out on the dark and roiling sea.

Saeed whistles. "That's a view," he says. "I wonder if you can see the Citadel from here?"

Etheldreda moves noiselessly toward a door on the far side of the room. She pulls out a long iron key. "I stole it from Javid's ring this morning. He doesn't like carrying it around, so he leaves it on a hook in the kitchen."

As the key turns, there's a loud click that seems to echo through the room. "Hurry," you cry, sprinting across the dining room with Saeed into the office beyond. The three of you crouch in the room, waiting to hear if the loud click alerted any of the guards.

"There won't be any guards in this part of the house," Etheldreda avers. "There are two posted at the front door, so there won't be any on sentry inside."

After a minute of listening to your own heartbeat pounding in your ears, you relax. No one heard you. Etheldreda rises and turns a key at the base of a wall sconce. A pale flame comes to life inside a glass globe.

"Whoa," says Saeed, his eyes widening.

"It's a torch that ignites when you turn the key. There's some kind of spirit-air, and the spark lights it," Etheldreda explains. "Only the nobles and the King are allowed to use it."

You look around the room, which looks like a normal sitting room to you. There is a divan and several chairs, and double doors that open out into a garden folly, with a hedge maze beyond at the edge of the cliff, shining green and silver in the moonlight.

"She's moved it!" Etheldreda cries. "The office isn't here anymore!"

"We could still search," you say, doubtful.

Saeed is listening at the keyhole. "Whatever you do, do it quick," he says. "Those men came up from the docking cave. I can hear them moving around in the kitchen."

"You can hear that far?" Etheldreda asks.

"Whisperer training," Saeed says sententiously, pointing a finger to his ear.

"There might be something around here," Etheldreda mutters, but it seems unlikely to you.

If you want to do a quick search of the room, go to section 35.

If you want to cut your losses and make an escape, go to section 38.

SECTION 15

You turn and creep back up the spiral staircase. As you reenter the manor house, you see the kitchen is brightly lit and you hear voices. You hurry into the kitchen and stop short.

Saeed and Etheldreda are both there, held by guards, accompanied by the officious-looking castellan, Javid.

"Well, well," he says nastily. "It seems that the third musketeer has appeared. I imagine the Baroness will want to speak to the three of you in the morning. Tie them up in the carriage house with the horses," he barks to the guards. "And you," he says to Etheldreda. "I'd have imagined you to be more grateful to Her Grace for allowing you to stay on your maedaw's land."

Etheldreda looks down at the floor.

"Get them out of my sight," snarls Javid.

The guards take the three of you to the big carriage house and tie you and Saeed back to back around one of the main supports in the center of the carriage house. As they lash you, as subtly as you can, you take a long deep breath in. You hope Saeed is doing the same.

"Dannel," Etheldreda begs one of the guards as they lash her to one of the poles supporting the hayloft, "don't let them do this to us!"

Dannel flushes and looks away while the other two guards continue to bind her.

As they leave, Etheldreda sags, her hair falling into her eyes. "I thought he would help us," she says weakly.

You exhale and feel a shift behind you as Saeed exhales. You feel the ropes loosen just a little bit. "Listen, Krishi," says Saeed, "if I press myself really hard against the support, it should loosen your ropes even more and you can squirm out."

"Smart thinking," you say, "but you're smaller. I'll press against the support and you squirm out."

Saeed is small-boned and agile, and within a moment he is free of the crudely tied ropes.

Etheldreda whistles. "We're not counted out yet, are we, strangers?"

"Who are you calling a stranger?" Saeed asks with mock indignation as he goes to work on her ropes and you wiggle out of yours.

"All right, quick," you say. "We have got to make it back to the forest before they realize we're gone."

"I can't!" Etheldreda says, shocked. "I have to stay and try!"

"It's too dangerous," Saeed tells her.

If you insist on Etheldreda coming with you, go to section 17.

If you agree to stay and help, go to section 18.

SECTION 16

You ou recognize the prisoner's voice, and you have to figure out who it is. Stealthily you creep down the rest of the way. The stairwell opens into a cavern about twenty feet wide and about thirty feet long, where there is a broad shelf for pulling up boats, as well as a channel of water where larger boats can pull in. Just next to the stairwell are stacks of wooden grates and sacks, and you duck behind them.

A small yacht has pulled in. There are actually five men. Four of them are gathered on the beach. At their feet is the prisoner who was just struck. The fifth, somewhat smaller and slighter, is bent over the lines, lashing the boat to a stubby mooring log driven into the strip.

The prisoner slowly stands, insolent, dragging a forearm across his face where he was struck.

"Your mistress will not thank you for so roughly handling me," the young man snaps, his dark eyes flashing with anger.

Now you know where you heard that voice before.

It's Arjun.

But what on earth is he doing here in Two Rivers? And why would these men go through the trouble of bringing him in the dead of the night?

The leader of the men barks in laughter, "She don't mind what condition you arrive in, so long as she's the one with her hands on you and not anyone else. She can serve you up to the Narbolin with a bruise as well as without."

"You overestimate my value to the Baroness as collateral with the Narbolin."

"That's between you and her, isn't it, *Your Majesty?*" the pirate snarls.

Arjun. *King* Arjun, you slowly realize. If the Baroness has the Albahri King and an alliance with the Duke of Kulsum, this whole situation just got worse. Much, much worse.

Four men. With the element of surprise, you're sure you can take them.

"All right, boys," the Captain says. The fifth man has finished mooring the boat. He stands, his back still to you. "It's time to take our guest to his quarters. The Baroness can see him in the morning."

If you make your move right now, go to section 24.

If you stay hidden and see what happens next, go to section 25.

SECTION 17

"Etheldreda," you say, "no one is going to contest that your claim is serious, but there's nothing else we can do here. We lost, all right? We have to make a break for it. We'll come up with a plan, I promise. And we'll fight another day."

Etheldreda wrings her hands, tears coming to her eyes.

"All right," she agrees. "Let's go."

"Have you ridden bareback?"

She nods.

"We'll take horses then," you decide quickly. "We'll lead them out as quietly as we can, and once we're to the main road, we'll mount and run like hell."

"First," Saeed says, his eyes twinkling mischievously, "I have a little mechanical work to do." He scurries under one of the carriages and starts slashing with his knife.

"Smart," says Etheldreda, pulling out her own belt knife and making her way to where the tack hangs.

After Saeed has sabotaged the carriages and Etheldreda has cut through the harness and reins, the three of you lead horses as quietly as you can out of the carriage house and down the path past the manor. You're about halfway down when out of the darkness comes a cry.

"Who goes there?"

The soldier comes forward, and you can make out his white face in the dim light from the stars and the moons.

"Dannel!" Etheldreda calls. "Dannel, we're leaving."

"I can't let you," he says thickly.

She hands her reins to you and walks up to Dannel, putting her hand on his forearm. "Take me back then," she says softly. "But let these two go. They'll get help."

Dannel looks at you, his expression stricken.

"Etheldreda, no," you say. "This is a bad idea."

"It's not your decision to make, Whisperer," she says sadly. "I cannot leave. This is my land. Its fate is my fate. Dannel won't let them hurt me."

He reaches up then and puts a hand on her shoulder, but not to detain her. It is a protective gesture.

You shake your head. You doubt the Baroness will be so lenient, but Etheldreda has left you no choice. You and Saeed mount your horses and ride hard for the forest. As soon as you reach the main road, you hear cries from the house and know the guards have been alerted.

You don't look back. The forest is dangerous at night, but with any luck you'll make it to the Farmhouse by dawn.

THE END

SECTION 18

"All right," you agree. "We'll stay and help."

"I can still get into the house," Etheldreda says. "The kitchen entrance isn't the only way."

"What other way is there?" Saeed asks dubiously.

Etheldreda looks beyond you at the manor's grand entryway, one of her eyebrows raising.

"You want to go in through the front door?" you ask, surprised.

"Why not?" she responds. "No one expects it. There won't be any guards in the foyer of the house."

"But there will be in front of the house."

"You must have some Whisperer tricks up your sleeve to deal with a couple of cut-rate guards. They're not trained militia! Some of them are practically kids themselves."

"All right, all right," you say. "Let me think."

"We can take them!" Saeed says with relish, punching one tiny fist into a little palm, making smacking noises.

If you want to fight, go to section 19.

If you think it's better to sneak in, go to section 20.

SECTION 19

"We can handle them," you say decisively. "We'll stay in the shadows. Saeed and I will creep alongside the house, and Etheldreda, you circle around to the main walk. When we're in position, we'll give a signal—"

"I can hoot like an owl," Saeed volunteers.

"Good as any," you agree. "Then Etheldreda, you walk right up to the door. The guards will react either by talking to you or by trying to apprehend you again. That's when Saeed and I will strike!"

Saeed tries to make a menacing face and draws his rigid fingers across his throat in a slashing gesture. "And then those mooks are TOAST!"

Etheldreda stifles a smile. "All right, and then what?"

"Then you get in," you say, "get what you need, and get out. Saeed and I will wait at the door for you. As soon as you're out, we make for the trees."

Etheldreda nods curtly, and three of you steal from the carriage house. You make a sharp gesture and she peels off down the carriage drive, while you and Saeed tiptoe past the kitchen entrance and then veer in, staying close to the house itself.

You sneak among the bushes and approach the main portico, blocked from view by the large glittery pillars. You look out to the yard to see if you can spot Etheldreda in the darkness. It's impossible to tell where she is, so you just look at Saeed and shrug. He lifts his hands to his mouth and hoots. He's pretty good, actually!

Just on cue, Etheldreda steps into the light.

"Gentlemen," she says casually.

"Etheldreda!" calls out the younger of the two guards. It's Dannel, the guard she implored earlier.

She stops. *Uh-oh.* You gesture frantically to Saeed.

The other guard is stepping forward when suddenly Dannel grabs his jerkin and twists him back around, swinging wide with a left hook that connects solidly. Saeed's mouth opens into a little 'o.' "Nice punch, brother," he drawls when the second guard collapses in a heap.

Etheldreda's hands fly to her mouth.

Dannel pulls the inert guard into the shadows. "I don't know how long he'll stay out for, but I think I just cooked my own goose."

"No," she says, rubbing his arm, "we'll protect you."

"Get in there, Etheldreda," you warn. "Get in there and get the papers you need. We need to get out of here as soon as we can. Take Saeed with you. Dannel and I will keep lookout."

Saeed and Etheldreda disappear into the house, and you regard Dannel for a moment. You think about the way Etheldreda comforted him and decide to trust him.

"You know what's going on here?" you ask.

"I can guess," Dannel says, the worry not leaving his face.

"Then you know you have to get Etheldreda out of here as soon as she comes back. Saeed and I will stay and try to create some kind of delay. You need to get her to a place called the Farmhouse, and when you get there, ask to speak to master Shivani."

He nods numbly while you give him terse directions to the Farmhouse.

"Now go saddle up two horses and lead them quietly down the drive. You're going to have to take this guy with you," you gesture to the soldier Dannel knocked out.

While Dannel goes back to the carriage house, you pull the soldier across the lawn to the carriage drive. On a whim, you pull off his uniform, both the jerkin and cap, and pull them on over your own clothes. As long as Javid doesn't see you, you might be able to blend in with the other guards for long enough to pull off your own escape.

"Krishi!" You hear a call from the doorway. Etheldreda and Saeed are standing there.

"I'm here!" you hiss.

They come through the darkness before you.

"I couldn't find the Duke's letters," Etheldreda says. "But I know how they're smuggling weapons in and where they're going."

"That's a good start," you say. "Shivani will know what to do."

Etheldreda suddenly notices Dannel coming down the drive with only two horses. She looks at you with a question in her eyes.

"You guys head out first," you say brusquely. "Dannel knows where to take you. Saeed and I will stay behind just long enough to make sure you're not being followed. We'll be right behind you, I promise," you reassure her.

Dannel looks at the inert soldier. "Don't worry about him," you say. "We'll drop him off in the forest once we get far enough away from here. He'll be fine."

As Etheldreda and Dannel mount and ride off in the night, you turn back toward the house. With any luck, everyone will sleep through the night and it will be dawn before anyone goes to check on the prisoners supposedly tied up in the carriage house.

You swallow hard, waiting through the long minutes to see if anyone sounds an alarm. It was a risk staying behind, but it gives Etheldreda the best chance of reaching the Farmhouse.

"Don't worry, Krishi," Saeed says, patting your arm. "You made the right decision."

"I hope you're right," you say. "Come on, let's get our horses and get out of here!"

THE END

SECTION 20

"**I**f we're going to do this," you say, "we're doing it with the least amount of activity as possible."

"I can get you in," Saeed says confidently. "Watch for my signal."

"How will we know it?" Etheldreda asks.

"Trust me," Saeed says grandly, opening his arms wide.

The three of you creep past the kitchen entrance, and then Saeed gestures the two of you out into the lawn.

You crouch down in the darkness as Saeed inches his way closer to the porch. What is he planning? It's too late to ask now.

Then Saeed stands up and strolls right into the light. The guards straighten up in surprise.

"Gentlemen," he says politely, then breaks into a full sprint across the lawn toward the forest.

"Get him!" shouts the first guard. "I'll check the carriage house for the others!"

And just like that, both guards run off, leaving the doorway exposed. You and Etheldreda exchange a glance and then bolt for the door.

Once inside, you stop, catching your breath. As Etheldreda suspected, the foyer is dark. You pause for a moment, listening. From the kitchen you hear sounds, so you gesture to her quickly, pointing to the other part of the house.

"But the office is that way!" Etheldreda says.

"There's no time," you hiss, grabbing her wrist and pulling her down a short hallway into another room. You shut the door with a click.

You turn around to find you are in a room about fifteen square feet, with glass doors opening out onto a terrace. There are comfortable couches, a shelf lined with books, and a desk at the far end.

"She's moved the office," Etheldreda says with surprise. "This was the music practice room when I lived in this house."

"Quick," you say. "Check the desk. I'll watch the door."

Etheldreda makes her way around to the desk and starts pulling on drawers.

"They're locked," she snaps. "My maedaw never had locks on the drawers!"

"I guess things have changed a little," you say.

"Can you pop a lock?" she asks.

"I can try," you say, pulling the slender hairpin from your topknot and inserting it into the lock. You jiggle it. "It's not giving."

"Don't you have training?" she asks scathingly.

As you jiggle the pin again, you start sweating.

Footsteps pound down the hallway and the door is flung open. The two guards from the front door enter, huffing, and Javid is right behind them.

"This is getting to be a bad habit," he spits at you. "Your little friend got away, but we'll take better care of you this time. Lock them up in the root cellar," he says.

"My lord, it is cold there," protests one of the guards, who you recognize as Dannel, the guard Etheldreda implored in the carriage house.

"They'll survive," Javid says darkly.

As the guards hustle you down the stairs, you know you will not have another chance to escape. *At least Saeed got away*, you think. If you're lucky he will find help.

Though as you hear the heavy padlock to the cellar door clang shut, your hope fades into the night.

THE END

SECTION 21

"**W**ell done," says Sandhya when you tell her you summoned the storm and lit the beacon. "Senior students who have learned Elemental Affinity with fire, step forward!"

Seven or eight of the oldest students step forward, at the ready.

"We are going to draw fire down from the beacon in threads. The rest of you, all I want you to do is make channels in the rain from here all the way down to the ships. You can draw the rain apart, like so." She makes a little gesture with two hands, as if she is parting curtains, and you see a channel open through the misting rain.

"And then the fire-throwers can send fire through the channels like spears or arrows," you say. You think of the tapestry showing the flames being thrown down.

"Right," says Sandhya. We'll be far more precise if you aim the channels to carry the fire down for us."

"What do you want me to do?" asks Arjun, knowing neither how to part the rain, nor how to call down the fire.

"You're the commander," says Sandhya simply. "You stand up there." She points to the landing on the staircase that leads up to the beacon. "And keep your eye on the whole battle. You command us where to concentrate the fire."

The students pair up, with one person parting a channel through the deepening storm, and the other person drawing fire down from the lit beacon in orange lashes. Arjun steps onto the landing.

There is a thundering boom. The ships are launching projectiles at the walls of the Citadel! At Arjun's shouted command, the Whisperers launch fire back as the channels are created.

The walls shake from impact.

"Turn your fire to the left-most vessel!" shouts Arjun. Pedro, a senior student, launches a projectile into the foresail. The rest of you launch fire-spears in that direction until the boat is immobilized, its sailors scrambling to save their ship.

As you continue your assault, Arjun focuses the attacks, first on one ship, then the other. Soon all four ships are aflame and stalled. Two of the crews have abandoned ship and are scrambling aboard the rocks of the breakwater.

The Narbolin soldiers who eventually burst onto the rampart walls are soggy and demoralized. When faced with a wall of Whisperers brandishing both fire and rain, they drop their weapons and kneel in surrender.

Sandhya approaches the kneeling soldiers. She opens her mouth to address them, but, having made some kind of decision, closes it again and gestures to Arjun.

To your surprise, Arjun straightens, descends the staircase, and approaches the soldiers.

In a severe tone you haven't heard him use since the first night you met him, Arjun says, "You have attacked a place protected by Inviolate treaty. If your master accepts responsibility for you, the sanctions on him will be extreme. I imagine that he will not accept responsibility for your actions today, in which case it will be you that suffers the punishment of the treaty violation, perhaps even by his hands."

"Ah, the irony," a soldier at the end of the first line drawls irreverently. "Touché, Your Majesty," he says, rising from his knee off the ground only slightly, so he is in a deep, deep curtsy. "You have won the day and got the better of us."

"Captain Zephyr," Arjun says crisply. "There's only one way out of this now. You will release your men to be prisoners of master Sandhya at the Citadel, and you and a crew of my own choosing will bear me and my attendant"—Arjun gestures toward you—"to Albahr, where we will have words with the council about the Narbolin Emperor's treacherous breach of Inviolate treaty!"

"If there's a ship left that isn't burned," you mutter. The demands of the day, coupled with this surprising reveal of Arjun's true identity as the King of Albahr, have you nearly speechless.

Arjun slaps his forehead in exasperation. He turns to Sandhya with a pained expression on his face. "Master?"

Sandhya nods her assent with a smile and turns to the storm. You watch as she raises her hands overhead and draws together acres of rain. It forms a huge ball of water and then releases in directed snakes and streams. The burning boats are extinguished. The sailors who had managed to finally reach the top of the breakwater fall back out into the harbor. Coughing, they once again begin swimming for safety.

"Ah, sorry lads!" Sandhya cries down to them, shrugging her shoulders in pretend helplessness.

"Stand, Captain Zephyr," Arjun orders. "You're under my command now."

The gray-eyed Zephyr smiles, rises, and bows his head just slightly. "I am, Your Majesty," he says simply.

"To Albahr then. The Citadel is safe and the Narbolin will answer for his crimes."

THE END

SECTION 22

"Krishi!" Sandhya calls out. "Where have you been?!"

"We went to the Heart of the Storm and called in a typhoon to block the Narbolin ships!"

"You did what?" Sandhya is clearly alarmed. "Krishi, the stone is ancient and charged with incredible power. You could have really hurt yourself!"

"I was there," says Arjun calmly, stepping up beside you to face your teacher. "I supported Krishi during the spell."

"It was a miscalculation," she snaps in irritation.

Good. You like annoyed Sandhya better. Worried Sandhya was really frightening you.

"You!" Sandhya calls out to one of the senior students. "Gather all the students below and as far to the interior of the Citadel as you can get!"

You are about to protest that the waves wouldn't reach this high when there is a huge clap of thunder and a wave crests against the battlement. You think you hear the shattering of windows below. You turn to join the other students under the shelter but Sandhya grabs you roughly by the shoulder.

"Not you, Krishi. You're coming with me to watch this. You too," she hisses at Arjun. She strides over to the battlement edge, drawing her drenched cloak around her in a useless gesture.

Your shoulders droop. As you are about to follow, Arjun takes your hand. You look over at him. "I'm here with you," he says. "I encouraged you. I will share your punishment."

The three of you cling to the parapet and strain to see through the rain. You hear Sandhya whisper strange syllables. You can only see the sea ahead of you in flashes through the rain and clouds. The wind lifts the mighty ships up and flings them against the breakwater. The ships break on the stones.

Men cry out for rescue as they scrabble to climb up on the massive boulders of the breakwater. At the first sound of a crew member's voice, Sandhya turns and claps her hands loudly. When she speaks, her voice sounds out against the storm. The storm ends, its sudden absence almost as dramatic as its presence was.

Slowly, the students of the Citadel come back out of their shelter. Sandhya watches them with a still calm.

"That's it, students. When the first man asked for aid, the ancient law of Sanctuary was invoked. Everyone, report to your chore section. Senior students, follow rescue-at-sea protocols. Continue to still the storm. Bring these men in. Confine them to the docks please," she declares, clapping once again forcefully and sending the students skittering to their orders. "Not you two," she says again, deftly plucking the backs of your shirts as you try to make a quick escape.

"Krishi, this is a problem. We attacked first. It's against the Code of the Whisperers."

"I will take responsibility," says Arjun then. What is he doing?

Sandhya slowly swivels toward him, fixing him with that gaze you and your friends always cowered beneath. "Will you?" she asks, her voice low and edged with danger.

"I will," he says, raising his chin and staring back at her. You gulp.

And then, to your shock, Sandhya softens. "This accelerates everything, Your Majesty. We were not prepared for a direct confrontation with the Narbolins—"

"I'm sorry, what now?" you say, raising your hand.

Arjun turns toward you, a small smile of regret on his face. "It's me, Krishi. I'm the King of Albahr. I didn't vanish. Dev brought me here to keep me safe. No one but Dev, Chandh Sahib, Suraj, and Sandhya knew. And now you. We have to be able to trust you, Krishi."

"You can trust me," you stammer. "But what happens next?"

Arjun exchanges a long look with Sandhya. "I'm not actually sure. We don't know whether Dev's mission has succeeded and whether it will be safe for us to return. We also, as Sandhya said, have a cavern full of prisoners. Or refugees. Or whatever we should call them. It's a diplomatic mess though, that's for sure."

"We'll figure it out, Arjun," you say, taking his hand. "I am here with you."

"All right," says Sandhya briskly. "But first things first. We have some prisoners to rescue. Or new visitors to greet. But whatever they are, we need to get them warm. And fed. So we can talk to them. With a few drops of truth-flower tincture in their supper wine, perhaps?" she says, with a wink that belies the worry you feel.

THE END

SECTION 23

$\mathcal{S}$andhya thanks you curtly for lighting the beacon, then moves to address everyone.

"Students!" Sandhya commands, and the whole group of older students is all ears. "Those of you who have practiced an elemental affinity with fire, gather around. We are going to draw energy down from the beacon and use it to attack the ships!"

"And the rest of us?" you ask.

"The rest of you watch the stairwells. If ground troops enter the Citadel, they will definitely make their way up here first instead of looking for prisoners. At least there's that to be grateful for."

"You're trying to draw their fire," you say. "You're not fighting to win."

A rueful look comes across her face. "There are too many of them, Krishi. The best we can hope for is that Suraj got the children to a good hiding place."

You hear a crash. The ships are firing at the Citadel walls.

"To the fire," shouts Sandhya, and students begin drawing the fire down from the Citadel in spindly threads and with various levels of success, coalescing them into globes and hurling them down toward the galleons as they fire at you.

You appreciate Sandhya's strategy. Even though most of the students can't aim carefully enough to strike the boats, the odd globe lands close enough to keep the sailors distracted and occupied with keeping their vessels safe.

The fight is short, but spectacular. One galleon's main sail is consumed in a conflagration. But your efforts are not enough to disable the ships.

Eventually, as Sandhya predicted, a score or more soldiers burst onto the courtyard. You try to bar them from arresting the fire-throwers, but a handful of unarmed junior Whisperers using techniques they have only recently learned are no match for battle-hardened professional soldiers. Within minutes they have overwhelmed you and apprehended Sandhya and the senior students.

"Someone put out that beacon!" roars the Captain. Two soldiers run for the staircase, and Sandhya nudges Arjun into the back row of students and steps in front of him.

The soldiers part to let through their commander, a slight and slender man with long silver hair, brandishing an evilly curved blade. "Ah, the Whisperers. Up to no good, as always," he drawls.

"You attacked us," snaps Sandhya. "You breached walls protected by Inviolate treaty!"

"Is that so?" he asks in an innocent voice. "Because what the

Narbolin Emperor heard is that the King of Albahr has been abducted. By a Whisperer. And brought here. Now, you wouldn't know anything about that, would you?"

Sandhya's eyes widen and she swallows. There is a long moment of silence.

"I was not abducted," says Arjun.

"Arjun, *no!*" Sandhya hisses.

You stare at him. He steps out from behind Sandhya.

"Your Majesty," purrs the commander, bowing low.

"Captain Zephyr."

His eyes open in mock surprise and he presses his hand to his chest. "One is known by the King of Albahr!"

"Only that you work for the highest bidder. I was not abducted," he repeats. "I came to the Citadel of my own free will."

"Oh, careful, Your Majesty," Zephyr says silkily. "To be brought out of the boundaries of your palace against your will is indeed a crime, but leaving the borders of your own kingdom without agreement of your own Privy Council could be considered abdication."

Arjun's face is stony and cold. Sandhya looks defeated.

"We will see about that when we return to Albahr!" Arjun snaps.

"Well, Your Majesty," Captain Zephyr says delicately, "if it's true that you were abducted, then certainly we shall deliver you to Albahr at once to consult with your council. But on the other hand," he pauses, "if you came willingly and abdicated your responsibility to the throne, I imagine we shall leave you here and bear the news back to the council that they must elect a new king."

You've been outsmarted. Arjun looks at you, something of an unspoken question in his eyes. You give a slight, tight nod.

"Very well, Zephyr. The ordeal of my abduction was trying. I will return with you under two conditions. First, that these people not be harmed but only kept prisoner. Second, I insist my attendant accompany me." And he pulls you—roughly—forward by the elbow. "Look alive, valet!" Arjun says to you severely. You pretend to stumble, allowing your hair to fall into your eyes.

To your surprise, Zephyr shrugs his shoulders and says agreeably, "Yes, Your Majesty. You must return to Albahr at once. My ships are at your disposal." He gestures toward them courteously.

Arjun squares his shoulders and walks between the columns of soldiers. Two immediately flank him. He may be the King of Albahr, but it is clear that he is also a prisoner. Zephyr cocks his head at you in a gesture to get moving. You shuffle along behind them, trying to act every bit the servant Arjun identified you as.

"Don't overdo it, Krishi," you hear Sandhya's voice flicker in your ear, as if she was speaking directly into it. "Royal attendants aren't drudges. In fact, they're often minor nobles themselves for whom the service is considered a privilege. Less is more. Goodbye, Krishi. And good luck." And her voice fades.

As you walk from the courtyard of the ramparts into the darkened stairwell, you cast a glance back and see the soldiers, pikes extended, circling the remaining Whisperers.

There's a whole sea voyage ahead, you reason. Plenty of time to think about how you're going to get out of this one, right?

THE END

SECTION 24

It's now or never. You take a quick look around. There's a coil of rope with a heavy hook at the end. It's as good a weapon as you're likely to find, so you grab it, slinging one end of the rope around your shoulder and holding the other end in your hand, the hook dangling loosely.

As the men begin to hustle Arjun toward the stairwell, you leap out from behind the crates, swinging the hook wide. The rope wraps around one of the men's waists, you give a mighty tug, and he stumbles.

The other men look over in surprise, and Arjun wrenches his arm free and makes a break for it, running toward the far end of the cavern.

"Not that way!" you shout.

The men roar in protest and whirl to face you. The man you yanked off his feet is pushing himself up, and he doesn't look pleased.

The smaller man by the boat throws back his hood. It's Zara! She must have been undercover! She's got an oar in her hand and she swings it wide at the men, all of whom have their backs to her. The oar catches one of them in the side of the head and knocks another two down as Zara continues her swing.

"Krishi, go after Arjun!" Zara shouts. "I'll take care of these men!"

If you run after Arjun, go to section 26.

If you stay and help Zara, go to section 32.

SECTION 25

You ou stay hidden for the moment. Your instincts tell you that there will be a better moment to make your presence known.

Four of the men hustle Arjun toward the stairwell. The fifth man follows them, then pauses. You freeze. He turns in your direction, then reaches up and slowly lowers his hood.

It's Zara! She holds a finger to her lips.

She turns back to the men.

"Captain," she says in a rasping, affected voice that you don't even recognize. "I must finish mooring the boat."

"Be quick about it, boy!" the Captain barks. "There'll be a lash for you if you tarry too long!"

The men disappear up the stairwell. Zara steals over to you. "Krishi!"

"Zara, what are you doing here?"

"Too long of a story to tell. The Duchess is out there, moored just past the craggy outcropping to the west. We have to wait until the men lock up Arjun, then we sneak back in there and break him out."

"We can't," you say. "Zara, Saeed is here. He's up in the house somewhere. We have to get him. We can't leave him behind."

She gulps hard. "All right, first one and then the other."

The two of you wait for several long minutes and then creep up the stairwell, waiting to hear if the men are there. As you leave the stone-cut tunnels behind, you enter the vestibule, where the staircase shifts from spiral hewn from the cliff rock into the regular wooden and stone construction of the house.

A half-flight above you, you hear the sailors in the kitchen, drinking ale and toasting one another. There's a door in front of you that must lead to the servants' quarters. You gesture toward it and Zara nods.

You pull the door open as quietly as you can and creep down the quiet hallway.

"They'll probably be holding Arjun in the regular quarters," Zara reasons. "I was listening to them on the boat, and he was really mad that the men were treating him like a hostage. He seems to think he still has some power in the situation. If he's right about it, the Baroness still wants to be on his good side. He won't be a prisoner locked up in chains."

"I don't trust him," you say. "Arjun's main priority seems to be Arjun."

"That may be true, but he's still the most valuable piece on the game board right now," she says. "Whoever has him has the most power. That's why Dev brought him to the Citadel. That's what this has been about since the beginning. I think we have to get Arjun back to Dev, no matter what."

"Saeed and Etheldreda were on the first floor. They're trying to find documents proving that the Baroness is working with the Duke of Kulsum to support the Narbolin Empire."

Zara lets out a low whistle. "Krishi, are we in over our heads?" she asks.

You reach the end of the corridor, where another staircase leads up.

If you go up to the top floor to find Arjun first, go to section 33.

If you stop at the main floor to find Saeed and Etheldreda first, go to section 34.

SECTION 26

$\mathcal{E}$ven though you are worried, you have seen Zara in a fight and you know she can handle herself. You run past the scuffle into the rear part of the cavern where Arjun disappeared. As you approach the far wall, to your surprise you see a crooked passage leading away. Ahead a light is bobbing in the distance.

You enter the passage and move as quickly as you can to catch up.

"Arjun!" you call out. "Arjun, it's Krishi!"

The light stops. You run and catch up. Arjun is standing there, his eyes wild, his glossy hair disheveled. You embrace each other quickly with relief, and you tell him you understand now who he really is.

"Dev brought you to the Citadel to protect you," you say. "Because you are the King of Albahr."

Arjun nods.

"I apologize for the deception," he says. "I trust *you*, Krishi, but you can see the situation is complicated. Already trust is being frayed. Those pirates knew my real identity, and they were willing to risk it all for a payoff from the Narbolins. Before the invasion, they would never have been so bold."

"What happened?" you demand. "How did they get you?"

"The Narbolins arrived at the Citadel right after you left," Arjun says. "Sandhya and Suraj and the others tried to fight, but they weren't prepared. Krishi, they have the Citadel now. I'm sorry."

You swallow hard at the news of the Citadel's capture. To mask your emotions, you look around the rocky crooked passage you find yourself in. "Where are we?"

"Smugglers' tunnels," says Arjun. "One of the barons must have had them dug in order to get goods into Albahr without paying the transit taxes. They're very old. When I was a little lad, my daw used to have dealings with the old Baroness. Her granddaughter and I used to play down here. I know these tunnels like the back of my hand. Come on," he gestures you down the passage. You go down a hundred feet or so and the path forks.

Arjun leads you to the right. "We always used to go to the left. Those tunnels lead under the lands and into the forest. There are a hundred little passageways, some of them natural from water channels and some of them carved to hide goods and trick anyone who tries to come down here. But this way," he gestures to the right passage, which seems wider, "leads along the cliff face and straight to Albahr."

"Where?" you ask.

He smiles fondly. "You know, we used to go all the time, but I was so little, I can't remember. I only remember that three men lived there and they were very kind. They used to give us spiced apples and then walk us back, scolding us the whole way."

"Well," you say, "I guess we are about to find out."

You walk down the passageway for what seems like hours, though it is hard to tell in the darkness. It's wide, wide enough for a person and a handcart, and on intervals along the passage are sconces with fresh unlit torches. You and Arjun transfer the fire as you walk along.

"Someone's been using the passageway again," you say. "Otherwise there wouldn't be fresh torches waiting for us."

"I believe I would like to have a conversation with the Baroness on that point," Arjun says darkly.

"Can't blame someone for trying to make a little money," you say slyly.

"I have a kingdom to run, Krishi," Arjun says with a sniff. "You'd be surprised how expensive it is just to have a road running through a forest for people to use. It has to be paid for, and you can't expect the poorest people to pay, can you? The rich merchants who are ferrying goods owe it to everyone else to make sure the road is good."

"Makes sense," you concede.

Eventually the passage comes to an end at a stout wooden door with metal rivets in it. You try the door, and though it is heavy, it swings open into what seems to be a small pantry. Various sacks of grain are stacked on shelves, and you smell the wheat ripeness of ale casks. Above, heavy boots tread the wooden floor.

You exchange glances with Arjun. His nose wrinkles at the sour smell of the casks. "Are we in a . . . tavern?"

The door at the far end of the pantry up a half-flight of stairs flies open, and a squat man with a delicately twirled pencil-thin mustache comes down the stairs gesticulating wildly.

"Another round of ALE they want? They've already finished a cask and now ANOTHER round?" He catches sight of you and stops cold. "Oh, what have we here? Visitors from Two Rivers, I imagine? Well, it has been quite a long time since we saw Dreda's wee buddy Archie, eh?"

"Archie?" you ask.

"Let it pass," Arjun says mildly.

"Welcome to The Three Roberts," the man says genially. He bows grandly. "I am one of the three. You may call me Robert." He pronounces the name in the Kulsumi style, with a flair and the final consonant silent: *ro-BEAR*.

"The Three Roberts," Arjun says excitedly. "This is one of Dev's touchstones."

"Touchstones?"

"He's charged the place up," Arjun explains. "The whole building is some kind of antenna. It's how Dev's spies talk to one another. You can use it."

You've never tried anything like it before, but you know that Whisperers can imbue—and access—energy. You kneel down, place your hands on the floorboard, and try to focus your thoughts the way you saw Chandh Sahib do when he was searching the ocean for the armada.

You close your eyes and listen to the city. You try to listen to all the voices at once. At first it is a cacophony of sounds, but slowly you begin sifting and discarding voices. You are immersed in a flow of voices in the district where The Three Roberts sits, and you travel street by street, away from the harbor and toward the palace.

Dev, you think. *Dev, are you there?*

And then, distantly but strongly: *Krishi?*

I'm at The Three Roberts. Arjun is with me.

Arjun is back in Albahr? Dev's voice in your mind is tinged with alarm. *Stay there. I'm coming.*

Sooner than you would imagine possible, Dev arrives with several other Whisperers. He takes you all upstairs to comfortable rooms in the inn. You tell him everything that has happened. His expression grows graver and graver.

"I am glad you were able to bring Arjun back to us," says Dev. "The Baroness and the Duke will be watched carefully, and we will take steps to prevent this from happening again."

"What about Saeed and Zara and Etheldreda?" you ask, sick with worry.

Dev's expression grows gentle. "I will see what I can find out, Krishi. We haven't heard anything yet, and that could be a good sign. Get some sleep, and we will face all this in the morning."

THE END

SECTION 27

ou cast your eyes about. There are four sloops pulled up against the shallows closest to the cavern's beachhead. You're guessing each carried ten soldiers.

It's not a big force, but it's big enough to secure the Citadel and too many soldiers for you to take on by yourself, especially not knowing what's happened to either Sandhya or Suraj. At least you got Arjun and the students to safety, but now you are on your own.

If there are forty soldiers here in the Citadel, then at least you might be able to cut them off from the boats still out at sea, beyond the breakwall. You make your way toward one of the sloops, though you have no idea how you'll launch it on your own, let alone sail it.

As you approach the sloop, movement catches your eye. It's a person! It must be a dockworker who hid under the canvas tarps. Or is it a trap?! You fall back into a fighting stance as the figure throws off the tarp and stands up straight.

"Going my way, Stranger?" drawls a familiar voice. The Duchess!

"What are you doing here?" you cry out in relief.

"I thought the Citadel might need my help," she says, pulling a stiletto out of her boot and holding it out to you, hilt first.

"Whisperers don't fight with weapons," you say. "Where are the others?"

"Whisperers fight with whatever's at hand," she retorts. "Frying pans, musical instruments, and yes, blades. I got the others to the fast-channel leading to Albahr and then I dropped into a rescue boat and hightailed it back here. Figured you were in for some trouble."

"Trouble found us," you agree.

"What's the situation?"

You like her mind. Tactical. Don't get caught up in too many abstracts: go straight for the details. "There's at least forty soldiers in the Citadel, I figure."

"You figure right," she says.

"And three galleons out beyond the breakwall if I make my count right."

"Four," she says.

You whistle. They're not good odds either way. Chance it here, chance it there.

"It's not a fair fight," the Duchess says. "But I thought that's what Whisperers were good at."

"And pirates?"

She winks.

If you think you and the Duchess should take
your chances at sea, go to section 85.

If you think it's better to keep the fight in the Citadel, go to section 86.

SECTION 28

"We have to take the chance and try to cause some damage to that fleet," you tell the Duchess. "What's your plan?"

She pulls the sail on the small craft as soon as you pass the breakwater, and it cuts starboard.

"We could try to stove the hull and sink the ship, but then there's a chance the other ships would be alerted to our presence."

"Unless they thought the ship sank because it crashed against the breakwater. What's the alternative?" you ask.

"You're not going to like it," the Duchess says. She pauses.

The rain is coming down, shielding you from the galleon as you approach.

"I'm ready for anything," you say confidently.

"We throw up a rope and scrabble up. In this storm the crew might be so busy keeping the galleon off the breakwater that we might be able to take out the Captain and the mate."

"But we'll still have the rest of the crew to deal with," you say.

The Duchess shakes her head. "The soldiers are probably all ashore. The only people left on the ship are the crew. The officers will be Narbolins, but I'd put pirates to ninjas that the crew are enlisted men, and in this storm they're cold, wet, scared, and dreaming of making it out of this alive. If we can put the Captain and the mates down, they'll take orders from anyone who can get them out of it."

"And that's you?" you ask.

She nods and stabs a finger in your direction. "And you."

If you want to try the Duchess's plan of commandeering the galleon, go to section 91.

If you think the risk is too great and you want to try to damage the ship, go to section 92.

SECTION 29

You take a deep breath.

"It's not wise to face such odds," you say to the Duchess. "We've done all we can here at the Citadel. We slowed the fleet and immobilized them. We got the younger students to safety. Suraj and Sandhya are doing everything they can. Now that we're free, our best chance is to reach Chandh Sahib and the others so we can let them know what's going on here and send reinforcements."

"All right," says the Duchess. "Good choice! If there's one thing I know, it's the fast-channels. You have to enter them exactly right, otherwise your boat just cuts across the current. With the right entry point," and she makes a sharp gesture with her hand against her forearm, accelerating it forward, "I can have us at Albahr before nightfall. It will be up to you to take the sail at my command."

You use several lines to lash yourself against the main mast as the Duchess takes the rudder.

"All right, Krishi, give it some wind."

You follow the Duchess's instructions as precisely as you can and your craft pulls hard aport, away from the bobbing galleons. The storm is intensifying. You take one last wistful look at the Citadel before it disappears in rain and fog.

"Ahead! Ahead!" the Duchess calls. "Get ready, Krishi, I'm tacking us in."

You feel a curious sensation as the choppy sea seems to still, and the boat seems to slow down to infinitesimal speed. Then suddenly, with a lurch, you latch into the fast-channel and the boat shoots forward smoothly and with accelerating speed.

"Cut the sail!" The Duchess calls out, and you do.

You turn around and face her, your eyes wide.

"You can release the lashes," she said. "In the fast-channel, there's no turbulence. It's a smooth ride."

You look out at the sea, whizzing past you, faster than you had ever thought possible. "How is this happening?" you ask her.

"The currents criss-cross the ocean. No one knows where they came from. Some think it's some kind of residual magic from when the islands broke free from the continents. Others think it's the work of sea-sorcerers. Only very few know the current maps. I'm one of those."

Incredibly, and true to her word, once you clear the storm, you see the shore of Elaria on the distant horizon.

"We'll cut out of the fast-channel before we get too close," the Duchess says. "No point in coming all this way if we can't sneak up on them."

"We can't go straight to the castle?" you ask, disappointed.

"I don't think it would help," says the Duchess. "I don't think Chandh Sahib is there. When the King went missing, the governing council took control. We think the Narbolin Emperor is pulling the strings. Let's lay low until we figure out what's going on."

As the light grows long, the Duchess cuts out of the fast-channel with a jolt. You approach the city, marveling at the great stone arms of the harbor that reach out from the south-facing city. The mouth is straddled by the largest statue you have ever seen, a warrior woman holding aloft a flaming beacon.

The Duchess whistles. "I never get tired of seeing that beautiful sight."

She steers the craft past the great cargo ships and passenger ships, past the smaller yachts and into what seems like the poorest and dingiest marina in the harbor. She slows to a drift alongside one of the great cliffs on the western side of the harbor. You follow a canal that leads into the cliff itself. After several minutes coasting through the dark, you pull up to a decrepit dock in a small cavern.

The Duchess leaps ashore and lashes the boat to the dock. A small, slender man with an enormous mustache emerges from the shadows.

"Duchess?" he asks, surprised.

"Roberto!" she cries out, and folds him in her embrace.

She turns and gestures you ashore.

You climb onto the creaky dock. "This is one of my oldest friends!" she says. "We'll be safe in his tavern!"

"Welcome to The Three Roberts," Roberto says to you. "I'm sure it's not how you planned your first trip. Chandh Sahib and Dev Acharya have been arrested by the governing council. They seem to think they were involved in a plot to abduct the King."

"Oh no," you say.

"Don't worry, Krishi," says the Duchess, worry filtering through the optimism she is forcing into her tone. "We will figure this out."

Considering everything you have already been through, you *want* to believe her.

THE END

SECTION 30

You turn your focus to the wood of the hull as you hack at it with the great hook. The more you try, the harder it is to feel any of the magic coursing through you. The wood of the hull reinforces itself, you slowly realize. It would be nearly impossible to sink a ship unless there was a huge impact. Trying to stove the hull was a miscalculation.

As you back away and try to reassess, there is a cry from above. The sailors have spotted you! The Duchess tries to get the boat turned around, but several sailors rappel down and seize you. You are restrained and brought up to the deck of the ship.

"Well, well," says the grizzled captain, coming down from the aft deck to face you. "What have we caught? A Whisperer and a Duchess. Oh yes, I know you, Madam. What would Zephyr say if he knew that we have caught and caged this little bird, eh?" And he pinches her cheek, cackling evilly.

"Zephyr is here?" she cries out. "Let me talk to him!"

"Oh no," he croons. "We all know what a weak spot the lad has for you, my Duchess. Methinks we shall clap you in irons straightaway and send you back to Albahr. The King's gone missing, don't you know, and the governing council is anxious to find those responsible. For some reason they think it's you. Some little bird must have told them."

"That's a lie!" you holler. "She was with me the whole time! She doesn't know where the King is!" But the Duchess shoots you a sad glance that makes your stomach sink.

He turns his attention to you. "Then you shall go in irons to Albahr as well, young Whisperer. See if they take mercy on you." With a sharp gesture, he commands the men to take you below.

You struggle mightily, but two strong men hold you tight. All the fight seems to have gone out of the Duchess.

Your mind works like mad. They're putting you in irons, sure. But they're taking you to Albahr. Maybe—if you're lucky—you can get a message to Chandh Sahib somehow. The moment is dark, to be sure, but all is not lost, not as long as you still have some fight in you.

THE END

SECTION 31

You take the hook in your hands. It is heavy, but not dense enough to make any difference against the hull of the ship. You can try to infuse it with some of your own life force, but it's risky. You know it would be easier if you had someone backing you up, supporting you with their own life force. You glance over at the Duchess.

"Oh no, my dear," she says, shaking her head. "Magic is not my ken."

You turn back to the hook, focusing your energy on it. You feel—slowly, atom by atom, it feels like—a transference between the hook and you. Your heart leaps. This is high-level magic! As the hook gets denser and heavier in your hands, you feel an exultation. But when you go to swing the hook, your own body feels heavier.

Oh no.

In the transference of your own essence into the hook, you failed to account for the fact that you would be displacing the hook's nature itself. Metal. Your own body gets heavier and heavier.

"Krishi!" the Duchess cries out in alarm, reaching for you.

Everything speeds up. She is there and disappears like smoke. Other beings come and go in a blur. Boats dock and launch.

At some point you realize it's not other people who have sped up but you who have slowed down, your body taking on the qualities of the durable iron. In a daze, you wonder if anyone will realize you are still alive and figure out a way to release you.

For many hundreds of years, sailors marvel at the lifelike qualities of the statue of the Whisperer crouched on the dock in the harbor with a hook in its hands. Some even swear they see its eyes move to follow them as they walk.

THE END

SECTION 32

"I won't leave you," you shout and leap into the fray. Between your quick kicks and Zara's wide-swinging oar, you make short work of the men.

With some of the lines, Zara ties the men up, back to back in pairs.

"Now, where did our boy king get off to?" she muses.

You head to the darkened recess of the cavern where Arjun fled.

"Well, look at this," you say, gesturing to a crooked passage that opens up at the end of the cavern. You take one of the torches from the sconce at the door and light it with your flint.

"Smugglers' tunnels," Zara says, and the two of you advance into the darkness.

Wherever Arjun was heading, he's long gone.

"What happened?" you ask her in the quiet darkness.

"I was with the Duchess on the *Blade*," Zara explains. "We were trying to stop the smugglers. One ship tried to run us, but they didn't make for the remote coast, they came in this direction, toward the headlands. The Duchess figured they had bigger plans than smuggling weapons, because why would they bring them in so close to the Albahri harbor? So I snuck aboard and replaced their cabin boy. They'd never looked twice at him anyhow so they never even noticed the difference!"

"Where's the cabin boy now?"

Zara shrugs. "The Duchess has him. Little guy, name of Pip. She's taken a liking to him. Dressed him up in a little waistcoat and breeches, same as she wears."

"All right," you say, pausing. "Where are we now?" You shine the torch one way and then the other. "Did we miss a turn?"

Zara shrugs. You press on, but your torch is getting dimmer. Passages open before you and you try the trick you'd learned once: always turn in the same direction, and eventually the path will lead you out. In this case, since you are holding the torch in your right hand, you decide to go left. You keep turning, but the hours roll by, and the torch eventually sputters out, and you and Zara are left in the darkness.

"Krishi, what do we do now?" Zara's voice comes to you from the darkness, tinged with worry.

"I don't know," you confess.

The only thing to do is keep going, and so you do.

THE END

SECTION 33

"**W**ell, whether or not we know or care about his agenda," you determine, "King Arjun has to be the first priority. Saeed and Etheldreda will have to take care of themselves."

You climb the staircase to the second floor. The stairs exit into a broad hallway that runs the length of the house. You can see the middle portion is open to the floor below, on one side presumably the foyer and on the other side the dining room or ballroom.

You gesture Zara down to your left, away from the open portion of the hallway.

"What now?" she asks. "Do we just start checking doors?"

You hold your finger to your lips and then tap your temple. She nods in understanding. You turn to the doors that line the left side of the hallway and cast your mind out. You remember what Arjun's mind feels like from when you read him at the dinner. You know people can shield their own minds, but Arjun won't be expecting anyone to be looking for him. Besides which, he has not trained to Whisper and you have.

Zara keeps watch as you slowly drift through the rooms, some of which are empty and at least one of which is occupied by someone you don't recognize. And then you feel a familiar presence.

"I found him," you say to Zara. "All the way near the end of the hallway. Third door down."

You hurry down, and Zara listens at the door. She looks up and shakes her head. You put your hand on the knob and she says, "No, wait! I do hear something. It's a pen on paper. He's writing something."

"Good," you say. "It means he's still up. Let's do this."

You throw the door open. Arjun looks up in surprise from the ornate desk by the window. The bedroom is richly appointed, the space dominated by a double bed with a canopy over it and heavy drapes that can be drawn around it.

"I told you he wasn't a prisoner," Zara mutters.

"Arjun! Are you all right?"

"I'm writing to Dev," he says. "The Baroness is planning to—"

"We know," you cut him off. "We don't have time to—"

"No, you don't understand," Arjun says, standing up. "They're going to—"

"STOP WHERE YOU ARE!" barks someone from the doorway. You whirl. The Baroness stands in the doorway in a scarlet sleep robe, flanked by guards.

"Your Grace," begins Arjun.

"Your Majesty," the Baroness says. "I apologize for this

intrusion. This . . . person . . . is a member of our gardening staff, accompanied here into the house by a lass who was the old Baroness's daughter."

Arjun's eyes widen. "Etheldreda is here?"

"I'm afraid so, Your Majesty," she says, and she steps aside, revealing two more guards in the hallway gripping a struggling Saeed and a shamefaced Etheldreda. "They were caught in the downstairs office, rifling through my personal papers."

Arjun's mouth opens in surprise. He looks straight at you with a cold expression. "Give me a moment alone with the young intruder."

The Baroness looks surprised for a moment, but then gives a little curtsy. "Of course, Your Majesty. Out! Everyone out! Take her!"

One of the guards grabs Zara and takes her out to the hallway. The Baroness gives you a look full of venom and then smiles tightly.

"We will be right outside the door, Your Majesty." She draws the door shut.

Arjun walks up to you. "I'm sorry about this, Krishi, but you've miscalculated."

"What do you mean?"

"I am depending on the Baroness to help me win the vote in the council against the Narbolins' proposed Writ of Accession."

"Arjun, she's not on your side, she—"

"It's King Arjun," he says icily. "I'm sorry, Krishi. When I get to Albahr, I will get a message to Chandh Sahib that you are being held here. I'm sorry I can't do more, but you shouldn't have gotten involved in this."

Before you can you say more, he strides to the door and throws it open. He gestures in the guards, then turns his back and sits at the desk again.

"It seems His Majesty is finished with you," says the Baroness. "Take him to the cells. He can join his friends and we will take care of them tomorrow before the party."

You struggle, but the guards drag you, Saeed, Zara, and Etheldreda down the stairs. Your mission is over.

THE END

SECTION 34

"Our loyalty is to our friends first," you say to Zara. "We have to make sure Saeed and Etheldreda are safe, then we can figure out how to handle Arjun."

You and Zara duck out of the staircase into a hallway adjoining the main foyer.

"Etheldreda said the Baroness's office was off the dining room," you say.

"That's it," says Zara, gesturing to big double doors off the foyer, opposite the grand front doors to the manor.

You slip into the darkened room. The long table has been set, and beyond it a wide window stretches the length of the room, open to the sparkling moonlit sea.

"Etheldreda! Saeed!" you call out in a low voice.

Etheldreda emerges from an archway on the near side of the room, next to the window.

"Krishi! We found something!"

"There's no time," you say. "We have to get out of here! Where's Saeed?"

"I'm here, Krishi!" Saeed pops out from behind Etheldreda. "Oh, Zara! You came!"

"We have to get out of here," you say. "*King* Arjun is being held upstairs."

"Arjun!" Etheldreda cries. "Arjun is here?"

"Yes," you say. "The Baroness had him kidnapped from the Citadel and brought here. We need to get you to safety first, and then Zara and I will go get Arjun."

"No," says Etheldreda. "I've known Arjun since I was a child. I need to talk to him."

"All right," you say, switching tracks. "Saeed, you and Zara get back down to the docking cave and signal the Duchess. Etheldreda and I will go upstairs and and fetch Arjun. If we're not down at the rocks in the next ten minutes, head out without us."

"We'll send help," Zara promises. The four of you reach the stairwell. Saeed and Zara peel off down the stairs, heading back to the docking cavern.

You look to Etheldreda to advise what to do next. This fine home used to be her domain, after all.

"If Arjun is upstairs, he'll be in the room at the eastern end of the corridor. It's the one reserved for visiting nobility and royalty," Etheldreda says.

"But he's a prisoner," you protest.

She shoots you a knowing look. "When you're a king, even if you're being jailed, the digs are going to be pretty nice. It allows the jailer to keep up the fiction of civility. Plus tides turn quickly. Trust me," she says, "I know how this game is played."

You steal up the stairs as quietly as you can. The upstairs hallway is empty. Etheldreda gestures you down the hallway to an ornately carved door. She puts her ear to the door and taps it several times. "Archie," she whispers as loud as she can. "Archie, it's Dreda!"

You hear footsteps, and the door is carefully opened. Arjun, his pale features gleaming in the moonlight, stares out in surprise. "Dreda, is that you?"

The two hug. "Archie, we have to go. We have a boat waiting," she says.

"Go? I'm not going anywhere, Dreda. The Baroness is helping me."

"That's what she wants you to think," you say. "But she's been working with the Duke of Kulsum this whole time. They're going to blockade the harbor when the Narbolin Emperor arrives. They're going to lay siege to the entire port until you sign the Writ."

Arjun's mouth opens in surprise. His gaze flicks from you to Etheldreda. "Is this true?" he demands.

She nods.

"I found documents downstairs that prove the Baroness is helping the Narbolins smuggle weapons into the countryside. We think they are arming insurgents inside the borders. When the Emperor calls upon them, they'll rise up. You're in danger, Arjun. We have to get you out of this house."

"All right," he concedes. "Let's go."

The three of you hurry down the hallway and down the

stairs. As you race down the hallway, Saeed appears at the top of the staircase leading down to the docking cavern. "Krishi! The Duchess is at the docks! Come on!"

As you make to follow Saeed, Etheldreda puts a gentle hand on your arm. "This is where we part ways, Krishi."

"What? You're not coming with us?"

She smiles sadly. "I can't leave, Krishi. This is my home. My work here isn't done. I'll sneak back to the dorms through the kitchen. You take the documents for proof," she says. Etheldreda crams the papers she's been holding into your hands. "Make sure you can do something with them. I'll be here, biding my time, working in the garden. Get Archie to safety."

"It's Arjun," he grumbles.

She smiles a big wide smile. "You'll always be Archie to me," she says, hugging him.

"I don't like this," you say, worried for Etheldreda.

"I'll stay," says Saeed suddenly. "I'll stay with Etheldreda."

"Really?" she asks, her face flushed with gratitude.

"Every Baroness needs a Whisperer by her side," he says, smiling, ducking in a little curtsy.

You hug Saeed tightly. "Be careful, buddy."

"I'm always careful," he groans, pushing you away and rubbing his eyes. "Now get out of here!"

You and Arjun descend the dark twisting staircase to the cavern. A runabout from the *Blade* has pulled up behind the pirate's sloop, and the Duchess's crew are loading the prisoners onto it and attaching great, thick tugropes to the sloop.

"Ahoy, Krishi," sings the Duchess from the deck. "It seems I've added a ship to my fleet! Best we set out to sea, eh?"

"Fast as we can," you agree.

"Will you captain the little ship for the time being?" the Duchess asks Zara.

"You bet I will," she says with a big grin.

"All right then," the Duchess says. "Choose a skeleton crew and head over to your ship, Zara. I need to stay here and keep an eye on these cliffs, but someone needs to get King Arjun to safety. With your permission, Your Majesty?"

Arjun says, "They're your ships, Captain, or should I say, *Captains*. Not even a king can countermand a captain's order at sea." He inclines his head toward the Duchess, and she gives him a jaunty salute in return.

While the Duchess sets out with the prisoners in the runabout, you, Arjun, and Zara scramble aboard the sloop. The sailors Zara selected from the *Blade* join you.

"Captain on board!" one of the crew sings out. "Orders, Captain Zara?"

"Neither the Citadel nor Albahr will be safe," you warn her. "We'll have to come up with another plan."

"All right, boys," Zara calls out crisply. "All hands on deck! Cast off the lines! Head out for open water! We have plans to make and precious cargo to see home safely!"

THE END

SECTION 35

"Let's at least try," you say, "so it's not a complete wash. But five minutes only. And Saeed, if you hear anyone getting closer, give the signal and we run."

Etheldreda starts poking around, checking a small bookshelf in the corner of the room and then opening the small drawers in each end table. "There must be something around here," she mutters.

You turn the key in the wall sconce, dimming the light. "I'm sorry," you say. "We'll have to work by moonlight."

Fortunately, the moons are so bright over the ocean that the room seems even brighter with the wall-flame turned off. Etheldreda stands then, holding up a letter and squinting to read it.

"This is it," she says. "It's a letter from the Duke of Kulsum! The Baroness is supposed to trick the King into believing she'll support him and keep him here for 'safekeeping,' but really she and the Duke will go to the council in Albahr and undermine him!"

"It's worse than we thought," you say. "We need to get that letter to Shivani!"

She folds it up quickly and slips it into her pocket. "I'm going with you," she says. "The Baroness won't go quietly, and I will need support if I am going to stand up to her. This evidence is explosive."

You nod and gesture to Saeed.

"I know a way out through the garden," Etheldreda says. She leads you out the door and down the short path toward the hedge maze, but instead of entering she swerves right. There's a path that leads between the outside wall of the hedge maze and the cliffs. "Stay close," she warns.

The three of you hurry down the path, the hedge maze blocking you from the sight of any who might happen to look this way from the house. The moons light the path white before you. About a hundred yards on, you come to the end of the hedge maze to a promontory that overlooks the great Bay of Albahr. Across the wide waters, the city glows in the dark, even though it is in the deep hours of night.

"What do we do now, Krishi?" Saeed asks.

"We head to Albahr," you decide. "Etheldreda's parents can hide us until we can make contact with Chandh Sahib or master Shivani."

It will be a dangerous journey, but it's your best shot.

THE END

SECTION 36

You look from Chandh Sahib's eyes over to your friends. You're a little afraid. The Citadel has been your home for so long—and it does feel like "home." The thought of it in danger while you are away is terrifying. But Chandh Sahib needs you.

"I think I should go with you," you say.

Chandh Sahib nods. Exchanging a glance with Dev Acharya, he says, "I will take my leave of you to make some preparations. Duchess?"

The Duchess rises from the fireplace, suddenly all business. "I shall prepare the ship. Meet me in the docking cavern within half an hour. There's no time to waste if we're going to slide into the fast-channel. We can avoid the Narbolins' detection while it is still dark. No point in being caught out of safe harbor when the sun comes up and all can see us!" And with that she strides off with Chandh Sahib, the two of them talking quietly.

The others in the room huddle quietly, except for Arjun, who lingers at the fireplace, staring into the flames.

"Are you worried about the King?" you ask him, trying to be friendly.

"Worried?" he asks you scathingly. "About him? The first sign that his country is in trouble and he turns tail and runs!"

"Enough," you hear Dev Acharya say severely. He strides over to where you are talking. Saeed and Zara lurk behind him, surprised looks on their faces. "It is not for you to judge your King."

"Isn't it?" challenges Arjun, defiantly meeting Dev's gaze.

You are astounded at his cheek! You realize, somewhat ruefully, that you will miss seeing this upstart when he receives the inevitable comeuppance he so richly deserves at the hands of Sandhya or one of the other masters.

"I suggest you retire for the evening, Arjun," says Dev Acharya in a smooth voice. "Things are happening this evening which do not concern you."

The boy, rather than showing any shame at what was clearly a rebuke from his teacher, turns on his heel and marches from the room.

Dev turns back to the three of you. "My children. Offer Arjun some latitude. He has left his family behind and is alone now in a strange place. Young Krishi, I believe Arjun is safe here with Sandhya. I am glad you will be coming to the mainland with us."

He turns and gestures to Sandhya, and the two of them leave the room also.

"Do not dawdle, young Krishi." You suddenly hear Dev's voice in your ear. Your eyes widen.

"Did you hear that?" you ask Saeed and Zara.

"Hear what?" demands Zara.

"We have to hurry," you say, and, taking each of them by a hand, you hurry from the room.

You, Zara, and Saeed pack quickly and then race pell-mell down the staircase to the docking cavern. You find a little party huddled at the pier, waiting to board the Duchess's ship. Some of the oldest and most talented students at the Citadel have been enlisted to join you. Somewhat to your surprise, the boy Arjun is there, talking with Dev Acharya.

All three of you are bundled up in traveling cloaks covering the nondescript tunics and leggings you wear. Saeed's mop of curls is hidden beneath a woolen cap, and with a start you realize that Zara has already chopped off her hair, and has it pulled back and pinned under so she almost looks like a boy. "I had to," she says with a grimace. "I stand out too much the other way. Now I'll blend right in."

"Welcome aboard the *Blade*, travelers!" calls out the Duchess from the ship rail.

"It's time," says Dev, walking up the gangplank.

You pause by Arjun, deciding maybe Dev was right. "Sorry to be leaving so soon," you say. "I bet it's hard to be left behind when so much is happening."

"That's just it! I don't want to stay cooped up here while you all go to Albahr!" His eyes flash with anger.

"We'll find the King," you reassure him. "I'm sure that he's doing what he thinks is right for his country. I don't think anyone who's a coward could become a king."

Arjun softens suddenly and gives the smallest smile. "Do you think so?" he asks.

"Yes," you say stoutly. "Without a doubt."

"Krishi!" calls Chandh Sahib from the deck.

"Got to go!" you cry out, giving him a clout on the arm, and then skip up the guardrail, your pack jouncing against your back as you run.

Deep belowdecks, in the narrow berth you were assigned, you come awake. It's pitch black, so you have no idea what time of night it is. Stealthily, so as not to wake your cabinmates, you get out of bed and pad into the main area. A ladder leads up to the deck. Silver moonlight pours down. You climb up onto the deck, and there at the port rail, peering out, are Zara and Saeed. You join them at the rail.

"Oh Krishi," Saeed says, turning to you, his eyes wide with wonder, "it's incredible!"

You look down at the water. The boat slices through at an amazing speed. The stars above shoot by. These fast currents cross several of the oceans, but their exact locations are closely guarded secrets. Navigation of the currents requires incredible precision. Many an intrepid captain has wrecked a ship trying to follow one of the water-roads, even after they've figured out where it is.

"They run under the water," says the Duchess, sauntering up to the three of you. "So if you look on the surface, you can't tell if they're there or not. Cut across them at anything but the most precise entry angle and you'll skip right over it. And if you manage to get into one, but don't know the precise way to exit one . . ." the Duchess makes an explosion sound with her mouth, flicks her hands open, and waggles all her fingers.

"WHOA!" you and Saeed cry in unison.

"So what are you lot still doing up?" she asks, leaning on the railing and pulling her flask out of her coat.

"What are *you* still doing up?" Zara asks the Duchess impudently.

"Ha!" the Duchess laughs. "I run this boat. I have to be up, so long as she's in the water-road, and then to navigate her out. Can't trust anyone else with that."

"How did you get your husband's maps?" Zara asks.

The Duchess takes a swig from the flask. "Stole them."

"Wasn't he mad?"

"Why do you think I'm working as a pirate captain instead of living in the lap of luxury, eating peeled grapes being served to me on a platter?"

"But still," Saeed says, "you wanted to be a pirate captain. That's why you stole the maps in the first place!"

The Duchess laughs again. "Laddie," she says, clapping him on his thin shoulder, "you do not know how uncomfortable it is to sit around all day corseted into a voluminous dress you can't even move in."

"Actually," Saeed says, leaning into her conspiratorially, "I kind of do."

As the Duchess promised, before the suns broach the eastern horizon, the galleon steers into one of the deep rocky harbors on the southern coast of Elaria, just west of the city of Albahr.

"All right, Whisperers," Dev Acharya says. "Time to cast ashore. There is an outpost of Whisperers inland called the

Farmhouse. I will write down the directions. The master there will instruct you in your duties."

You and Saeed pick up your packs and prepare to disembark. Zara doesn't move. She turns to Chandh Sahib then and says, "I want to stay."

"My child," says Chandh Sahib. "Dev and I must go to the palace and we cannot take you there with us. It's too dangerous."

"I don't want to go to the palace with you," she says. "I want to stay on the ship with the Duchess."

"I could find some use for a strong girl who wants to learn how to sail," the Duchess says casually, taking a long pull from her pipe. "And if you're right that the Narbolins are smuggling in soldiers to the countryside, wouldn't you rather have me patrolling after I drop you off in Albahr?"

Chandh Sahib looks at her for a moment, thinking. And then, to your surprise, he nods his head curtly. "And you, Krishi? Would you rather stay aboard and help the Duchess, or will you go with Saeed to the Farmhouse?"

If you decide to stay on board the Blade, *go to section 37.*

If you go on to the Farmhouse, go to section 48.

SECTION 37

After you bid adieu to Saeed, the Duchess drops Chandh Sahib and Dev off in another inlet closer to Albahr, just where the Bay of Albahr opens out.

"Follow those trails and you'll come to the Baroness Lowelia's estate. Her docking cavern opens out into the Bay itself. It's a short jump from there to the city!"

You bid Chandh Sahib and Dev farewell, and the Duchess begins calling out orders to her crew. The sails swell and the ship pulls away from the rocky inlet.

"Plenty of harbors just like that one all along these shores," the Duchess observes.

"And you know all of them?"

"Aye," she says. "I do. I know where the reefs are and where the water-roads are. Precious few there are who could outrun me and fewer still that could catch me if I were the one a-running."

"You're incredible," Zara says with undisguised admiration.

The Duchess laughs in a short bark. "Not incredible," she

says seriously, "just a woman who has places to be. Listen, friends, we'll pull out a ways and go down the coast to set anchor for the night. I don't want anyone to get wise to my secret hidey-harbors."

Since both you and Zara will take turns at watch, the Duchess sends you belowdecks to get some sleep for now. It seems like only minutes after you close your eyes that you hear the watch on duty, a young man called Pip, shout an alert. You and Zara jump out of your rope hammocks and climb the ladder up to the deck. The Duchess is on the aft deck behind the great wheel, a spyglass to her eye, scanning the dark western sky, the glowing lanterns at fore and aft barely piercing the thick fog.

"Someone's out there," she says, adjusting the glass. "I can see the running lanterns. What are they doing out this way?"

"Only smugglers would hug the rocky coast," Zara says darkly. "Or pirates."

"No matter which they are," you volunteer, "we should tread carefully since we're out here alone."

"Night's our friend, in this case," the Duchess announces. "Extinguish the lanterns!"

If you choose to engage the pirates, go to section 39.

If you decide to try some stealthy trickery, go to section 40.

SECTION 38

"There's no time," you snap. The last thing any of you needs is to be caught by the Baroness's militia on your first mission out as Whisperers. "Quick! To the garden maze."

"Wait!" Etheldreda calls, but you're already out the door, Saeed on your heels. You pelt down the garden path and into the dark opening of the maze, turning to look back at the house.

Etheldreda has not followed you! She's still in the manor, her shadow moving about the room, flickering in the golden light of the wall-flame.

"She's going to get herself caught," you mutter. "Come on!"

You and Saeed advance farther into the maze, taking first one turn and then another.

"How are we going to find our way out?" Saeed asks.

"That's not important now," you say. "This time we're trying to be lost. They won't think to look for us in here."

Eventually you find a corner to huddle up in. As the hours pass, you look up at the starry sky and try to account for your failure. You don't hear anything else from the house. Maybe Etheldreda managed to get away? You spend your time wracking your brain, trying to think your way out of the predicament you find yourself in.

You're not sure when it happens, but as you watch, the closest moon begins changing its phases, waning and disappearing and then waxing again to full. A whole month has passed and yet you have not slept, do not hunger, and have seen nothing but the night sky!

Many more months pass before you slowly and gently fall asleep.

THE END

SECTION 39

"We have to engage them," you say flatly. "All of Dev and Chandh Sahib's work is for nothing if the Narbolins slip past us now."

After a short pause, considering what you've said, the Duchess nods her agreement.

Running in full dark is more frightening than you imagined it would be. But the Duchess seems to have an uncanny instinct as to where the rocky crags of shore are.

"I don't want to pull out too far," she says, "lest the current take us and they slip by us in the night."

The other ship doesn't seem to be aware of you, though, as you get closer and closer to the bobbing lanterns of her lights.

"Krishi," says Zara, "how are we supposed to stop the other ship? The last of the sunlight's almost gone!"

"No worries, young friends," calls the Duchess from the aft deck. "This old pirate has a few tricks of her own up her sleeve!"

If you think the situation warrants your magic, go to section 41.

If you listen to the Duchess and trust her skills as a captain, go to section 42.

SECTION 40

"There's no point in blundering into something we don't understand. We're in safe waters right now; let's wait until they come to us. If they stop before they reach us, we can figure out what they're up to. If they keep coming, then it's them approaching us and we'll have the element of surprise," you decide.

The Duchess nods her agreement.

You wait until the sun sets fully. In the dark of night, you watch as the lights come closer and closer. You see eventually that there are three sets of lights. Before they reach you, they pull in closer to the shore and then the lights disappear.

"There must be another harbor," says the Duchess. "The whole coast is full of them."

"I have a plan," says Zara quietly. "What if Krishi and I sneak over in a small boat and try to board one of the ships? They won't expect us and if we're careful we can investigate and figure out who they are and what they're smuggling in."

"All right," agrees the Duchess. "But no risks. You get

over there and you do your investigation and you get out. No heroics."

In the deep of the night your little dory pulls up along the smallest of the three ships. You hear the men from the other ships unloading a cargo of crates onto a narrow sandy beach, the sand glittering silver in the moonlight.

You throw your grappling hook up and stealthily climb, hand over hand, to the ship rail and hoist yourself over. Zara is right behind you. You pause, crouching there, listening. All is silent.

"I don't think anyone is left on board," Zara whispers.

"Could we manage this ship on our own?" you ask.

"I think we could," Zara says. "At least well enough to pull it out from the harbor. And then we can signal the Duchess to send some crew over. Do you think you can call up some wind?"

There's a wind coming off the rocks and so you nod. Everyone knows it's easier to direct wind that's already there rather than try to stir some up from dead air.

If you want to commandeer the ship, go to section 43.

If you instead try to figure out what cargo the ship is carrying, go to section 44.

SECTION 41

*A*s you get closer, you see that there isn't just one ship, there are three! You're outmatched!

You look up at the lines of the sails. They glow with electric energy in the air. The energy is natural, but what you're about to do with it is not. Stepping your feet wide into the stance you learned, you raise your hands skyward and focus on its flame.

"Krishi!" the Duchess shouts. "What are you doing?"

There is a crackle as the light above you transforms into streamers of fire. You slice the air with your arms, cracking the lines of fire like whips toward the other ships. Their sails catch fire immediately.

"Fire at sea?" Zara asks. "A little overkill."

"Pull out," roars the Duchess, and the *Blade* tacks away from the course. The crews on the other ships start out frantically trying to douse the fire you started, but eventually they abandon the ships, setting off in little lifeboats, scrambling onto the crags and disappearing into the little inlets.

Sparks from the fire flash through the air.

The Duchess curses savagely. "Now we'll never find out who they were or what they were up to!"

"Duchess!" screams Pip from above, in panic.

"Kraken's hair!" swears the Duchess, as you all look up at the mainsail catching flame from the stray sparks.

"I'm sorry," you stammer. "I thought I was helping. They outnumbered us! We would have lost that fight!"

"Hard aport!" she calls. Turning to you with a grim look on her face, she snarls, "I don't suppose you can magic up some of those waves to put out the fire? Otherwise we'll all be swimming for shore soon enough."

"*I* can," says Zara, closing her eyes and bringing her arms out wide. As the water rises up in sheets, mist fills the air and surrounds the sail, dousing the flame.

The Duchess sighs in relief, then wheels around to face you. "Just because you have the power to defeat someone, Krishi, doesn't mean that that is the best course of action. We lost a valuable opportunity to discover what the Emperor is planning! Sometimes even being beaten affords a greater opportunity for success."

It's a lesson you wish you had learned earlier.

THE END

SECTION 42

The Duchess continues toward the light. As you pull closer, a ship materializes, though in the growing dark you cannot see whose flag they fly. The Duchess goes to the rail and calls out to the other ship. "Ahoy, sailors! In whose name do you sail?"

"It's no concern of yours, Captain," hollers a man from the other ship. "Keep sailing on if you know what's good for you!"

"I'm afraid I can't do that," she says. "In the name of the King of Albahr, I must ask you to announce yourselves and allow us to board and inspect your cargo."

"Fat chance," mutters Zara.

The man at the rail turns to say something to his comrades. As you draw closer, you see two additional ships trailing the ship you are addressing. You are outnumbered.

"They're bringing her about," you call to the Duchess. "They mean to ram us!"

"Ha!" says the Duchess, cackling. "That's what they imagine they are doing." She issues a stream of commands to her helmsman and then instructs you and Zara, "hold on to something solid."

You grab one the thick lines, and Zara seizes the ship's rail. The boat keels on a hard angle toward the shore and then back the way you came. The ship closest to you gives chase, drawing it away from the protection of the two others.

The Duchess seems undisturbed by this, and shortly you realize why. You hear the horrible sound of rock crunching through wood.

"That would be your keel meeting my favorite reef," the Duchess calls out to the other ship. "You have about ten more minutes, I will wager, before your whole ship is at the bottom of the sea, with the coral and the fish."

The other sailors run to and fro, but you can tell by the grim countenance of the sailor at the rail that the Duchess is correct.

"Of course," she says magnanimously, "I could offer you temporary respite on my craft. Provided none of you bring blades with you."

The other sailor hurriedly agrees and you and Zara help to throw a plank across. The sailors cross from their quickly sinking ship one by one.

"Now none of you better have blades on you," threatens Zara as they cross.

"Oh, I'll make a pirate of you yet," murmurs the Duchess approvingly.

Once the men, about fifteen of them, are on board, the lead sailor approaches the Duchess warily. "Now what?" he asks.

"What shall we do with them?" the Duchess asks you and Zara.

"Feed them, I suppose," says Zara.

"And let them have a bath?" you offer.

The Duchess turns back to the man, smiling. "And what do you have in exchange for those kindnesses?"

"We're humble sailors, my lady. We only carry what we're told to carry and where we're told to carry them."

"In this case, what would that be?"

"Weapons, my lady. Delivered from the Emperor of Narbolis to a certain harbor where we were to have been met. What happens to them after that, I have no knowledge of."

"Hm," the Duchess says, turning back to you and Zara. "What do you say?"

"He's not lying," you say. "He doesn't know where the weapons are going."

"Still, someone has to go and warn Chandh Sahib," decides the Duchess. "We go back to the harbor and we'll go ashore with the men as prisoners. We can make for the Farmhouse and leave them there and apprise Chandh Sahib of what's happening."

"And the *Blade*?" Zara asks.

"The *Blade* will need an acting captain while I am gone ashore," the Duchess says. "And I suppose that will have to be you." She takes off her giant three-cornered hat and plonks it on Zara's head.

"All right, boys," calls out Zara. "Set sail for the safe harbor!"

THE END

SECTION 43

As Zara pulls on the lines to position the sail, you raise your arms up and focus on the wind. It's an incredible feeling as your thoughts join the flow of energy in the wind. In a minute or two, you are able to subtly transition from flowing with the wind to bending the wind in the direction you want. The little ship begins to pull away from the other two.

There's a shout from the shore as the sailors realize what you're doing. The others scramble back to their ships, and one of the other ships gives chase.

"What do we do now?" you howl over the storm at Zara, but she doesn't have a chance to answer you. The other ship has rammed you and the deck keels wildly to the side. You are thrown into the cold and tempestuous sea.

"Zara!" you call out into the night, treading water as your limbs grow heavy. There is no answer but the roaring waves.

THE END

SECTION 44

"Stick to the plan, right?" Zara says.

You nod. "Get in, get out," you respond.

"I'll go below and check the hold," says Zara. "You see if you can see what's happening on the beach."

She disappears belowdecks, and you creep over to the portside rail and lean over to get a better view of the strand of rock on which the sailors are still stacking crates.

"And so we just leave them here?" one man says.

"That's what we do," the other one says. "Doron will be by to collect them. No one knows about this little inlet but us and him."

"And where does he take them?" another sailor asks.

"It's none of your concern, you two," the leader says. "Keep unloading."

"There's naught in this part of the country but canyons and cactus farms. Nowhere to go."

"Cactus farming is what you'll be doing to make a living, Nakul, if you don't shut your mouth. And your brother can go with you!"

The man called Nakul doesn't say any more, but sets to his work with a scowl on his face. You creep back to where your rope still hangs. Zara comes up from below.

"They've emptied the hold," she says. "But I saw the manifests. It's weapons. They're smuggling in weapons."

"And I know who their contact is," you say, "and I have at least some kind of idea of where they're storing them before they send them on their way."

The two of you climb back down to your boat and are off before anyone's the wiser.

"Good work, you two!" the Duchess says, smiling. "Let's get this information to the Whisperers! This is sure to put a wrench in the Emperor's plans!"

THE END

SECTION 45

"**I** can run the weapons into Albahr," you say casually.

"Aye, I'd say you can handle it," agrees Doron. "Casey! Finn! You go with Nakul. Alec, Caleb, and I will stay here and keep an eye on things," he adds darkly.

As Casey and Finn go off to hitch up the horses, you go back to your room with Saeed. "This is a bad idea," Saeed says. "We're not supposed to split up."

"You'll be all right, Saeed," you reassure him. "You're fast, you're strong, and you keep your wits around you in a fight. Just stay here, keep your eyes on those men, and keep Max close to you. If you can figure out exactly which cove they're bringing the weapons into and which trail they are using, then maybe we can get that information to Shivani and the Colonel and put a stop to this."

"And what are you going to do?" Saeed asks accusingly.

"I'm going to find out who these men are that are waiting for these weapons and where they are hiding. We have a real chance to foil this plot, Saeed. You have to stay focused."

Saeed takes a deep breath and nods. He looks at you, his face still scared. "You can count on me, Krishi."

When you come out of the room with your pack, the cabinet at the far end stands open and empty. In the yard, Casey and Finn have saddled up. A third horse is hitched to a two-wheel cart with a broad wooden locker on the back of it.

"You'll drive the supply car," says Doron. "You got a smarter head on your shoulders than this clown here," he claps Casey's shoulder affectionately, "and Finn's better in a fight, so better for him to be a-horseback in case you run into trouble."

"Trouble?" you ask.

"Albahri militia might be patrolling, but honestly, no one's going to suspect you coming in from farm country with a supply car. Your code word is 'sunshine,' all right? Don't forget it. That will get you in the door. You drop these off, hang around Albahr for a day or so, then you come back here for the next load. Just stick around the warehouse district in the city and don't get into any trouble."

"Yes, sir," you say, smiling reassuringly. You look past him to Saeed and Max, and then to the farmer, her husband, and their other son, standing on the steps looking nervous. How much of Doron and his crew's fervor does this family share? It appears that they'd like nothing more than to go back to farming cacti and be left alone.

The three of you head out on the cart trail, which rejoins the main road along Ribbon Creek. Rather than crossing at the bridge that would lead you back to the Farmhouse, you continue on through the forest.

The land becomes more inhabited as you enter the small

towns that surround Albahr. The broken land of the canyons to your right smooths out into wide fields that end in bluffs looking over the sea.

Briefly you wonder where Zara and the Duchess are now, and what is happening back at the Citadel.

Before too long, lost in your thoughts, you and the others have arrived at the Western Gate of Albahr. A florid-faced customs officer is bawling orders at whoever passes.

"Business in Albahr?" he demands.

"Bringing in prickly pears from the canyons," Finn says languidly, his hand straying near his sword hilt.

"More barking prickly pears?" he bellows. "The lords and ladies love them, don't they?" He waves you through.

"That was easy," you say to Casey.

"Easy?" Casey asks. "You didn't see the silvers Finn slipped him?"

You curse inwardly. You were so focused on Finn's sword hand that you didn't see what his other hand was doing. Dangerous mistake. Stay focused, you had said to Saeed. *You'd better do the same, Krishi*, you say to yourself.

Before long, you turn down a side street into a warren of alleys cutting through the warehouse district. Each one has a delivery dock. You stop at one, brown and nondescript. An imposing man stands on the dock next to a small door leading into the warehouse.

"How are ya?" Finn asks casually.

"Depends," the man says. "What do you think the weather will be like tomorrow? Dhoop or barish?"

Finn looks puzzled.

"You do speak Albahri, don't you?" the big man asks, casually hefting a stout cudgel.

Finn looks back at you, confused.

You say, "Dhoop." Go to section 46.

You say, "Barish." Go to section 47.

SECTION 46

"That's what I think too," the giant man says, observing the sky. "Sunshine for everyone." He steps back from the deck. "You can unload the materials and take them inside."

Casey and Finn remove the layer of prickly pears and unpack the parcels in the wood locker below. You step into the warehouse through the door that the big man is holding open for you. Inside the large space is an armory. Racks are filled with spears, swords, daggers, and maces. In the central area are long tables where a group of workers are fletching arrows. Past the main room are smaller rooms where you can see men moving about.

There must be a whole army in here! You notice a lofted sleeping area above you. The King will soon have an invading force popping up right under his nose inside the city walls.

Casey and Finn come over.

"Are you up for a tipple, Krishi?" Casey asks. "There's a tavern not too far from here."

"Yes, lads!" you say, trying to be jovial.

The three of you exit the warehouse and enter the dingy little tavern one street over, a whimsical blue and orange sign above it announcing, "Welcome to The Three Roberts." You wrack your brain. How can you get word back to the Farmhouse without raising suspicions?

To buy some time, you tell Casey and Finn that you will order the drinks. You approach the bar and a large, bluff man with a smart gray cap on his head greets you. "Hello there, friend! I'm Bobby and this is my place!" He pauses for a moment, scratching his chin and screwing his face up in concentration, looking up at the ceiling. "Well, it's at least one-third my place. There are two other Roberts."

You smile and order for the brothers. Bobby can offer you no food other than a sticky gruel which you politely decline. Your mind races, trying to determine your next move.

Dev. Dev can hear your thoughts and he must be in the city by now.

As Casey and Finn drink, they become raucous. You use a little trick you learned back at the Citadel, tipping your tankard, pretending to sip, but letting the liquid pour back into the vessel. Every once in a while when it seems no one is looking, you tip the tankard and let the liquid trickle to the floor. Soon you are staring off into space, pretending you are dazed. The brothers are singing a song with the table next to you, a song to health of the King. Ironic, that.

You close your eyes and focus. *Dev*, you think as widely as you can, as if you were shouting across the whole city. You wait. Seconds pass. Then a minute.

Krishi? comes a distant reply.

Dev, I'm in the warehouse district at a tavern called The Three Roberts. Come at once. The Narbolins have a secret enclave in the district and they are smuggling in weapons and men.

There is no reply, but you understand you have been heard. You exhale a sigh of relief and turn back to the brothers.

Casey flings an arm around you. "You're a good lad, Krishi. Good lad to have around. Isn't he, Finn?"

"Casey," you say. "Listen to me carefully. Go and have some fun tonight. Go to a good tavern in the merchants quarter. One that serves a nice meal. Take Finn. You've earned it, haven't you?" you press slightly with your mind toward him, trying to make the suggestion stronger. Casey smiles widely. It doesn't take much to convince him.

"That's a great idea, Krishi!" he says. "Come, Finn!" He corrals his bother. "Come, come!" The two brothers disappear out the door, arm in arm, singing off-key.

You push the tankard away from you and sit at the table, hands folded in your lap, waiting for Dev to arrive.

"Well done, Krishi," you hear a voice say. You turn and there is Dev before you!

"How did you get here so quickly?" you ask in a shocked voice.

Dev laughs. "Oh, a Whisperer has many, many tricks, young Krishi. Now, tell me where this warehouse is. The royal guard is standing by for my order. We will deal with the Narbolin threat properly."

THE END

SECTION 47

"Barish?" the giant asks, incredulous. His eyes narrow. "You're not from Albahr! What's your game?"

"I knew it!" swears Casey. "Doron told us to keep an eye on you!" He pulls his sword out of his sheath. "The code is 'sunshine,'" he snaps at the giant. "This one here," and he gestures his sword at you, "is trying to play tricks on us."

"Bad news," says the giant, hefting his oaken cudgel and swinging it wide.

You see stars. And then night falls.

THE END

SECTION 48

The Duchess and Chandh Sahib accompany you, Saeed, and other Whisperers ashore in a small boat. When you disembark onto the sandy beach, Chandh Sahib gives you hurried instructions. "Go inland through the forest trails. They are marked with a Whisperer's glyph which you should be able to recognize. When you get to the Farmhouse you will meet Shivani and the Colonel. They will tell you what to do."

"Goodbye, Your Grace," you say to the Duchess. "Please take care of Zara."

"It's me who needs taking care of, young friend," the Duchess says gaily. "And here's a parting gift for you." She presses a small velvet bag into your hand.

You pull the drawstring open and peer inside. The bag is filled with several handfuls of iridescent purple powder.

"Set it alight on the beach and I'll see the purple flames for miles in the dark. I'll come when you call," she says.

You say hurried goodbyes, and then they return in the dinghy and the galleon puts out to sea, the Duchess saluting you solemnly from the deck.

Remember, Krishi, you suddenly hear Dev Acharya say in your ear, *if you want to find, you must seek.*

By afternoon, after hours of hiking up through the forested canyons leading to the interior, you arrive at the Farmhouse, an attractive complex of buildings set in a hollow near the beginning of the agricultural fields of the Two Rivers District. Though the Farmhouse is a haven and school for Whisperers, it is also a working farm, an activity which disguises its true nature from locals and villagers.

You make your way across the main yard, where chore groups are huddled, distributing farm tools, talking about the afternoon's work. Across the quad, at the edge of the small wood bordering the fields, a large cabin stands. You enter it.

The interior is completely empty, and the walls are all lined with doors of various kinds and sizes, with different types of locks: some padlocked, others with doorplate and deadlock, and still others with mechanisms you have never seen before.

"For practicing pickpocketing," Saeed says in a loud whisper.

"Welcome to the Farmhouse," calls out an enormous woman dressed in a brilliant orange and pink sari, her hair in two long braids down her back, nearly to her knees. "I am Shivani, the principal." She turns to a small rail-thin man with an alarming shock of bright white hair. "Colonel!"

"Yes ma'am," he says deferentially.

"Fetch lunch for our new recruits! We must sit down immediately to discuss their missions!"

"Obliged, ma'am," he says, ducking his head. "Food is coming, ma'am," he adds as he scuttles away.

She looks after him fondly and then turns back to you, brisk and businesslike. "You'd miss him in a crowd," she says, "but this place wouldn't run without him."

As you sit, the Colonel returns, followed by a crew of Farmhouse students who serve you and your fellow Citadel students plates of rice and lentils with popped amaranth.

"There's good news and bad news!" Shivani booms as you eat. "We have finally received word that the King is safe. He went into hiding because there was an attempt on his life in the palace!" The room erupts in cries of alarm. "He is safe," she reassures the group. "For now."

The Colonel gestures for all of you to be silent, and after a ripple of protest runs through the room, everyone settles down.

"But here's the bad news. The Narbolins are infiltrating the countryside, buying off mercenaries and smuggling in weapons. If we want to stop them from taking advantage of the King's absence, we have to move quickly. I need volunteers."

Your hand shoots up first, followed quickly by Saeed's.

"All right," says Shivani. "All right, Krishi. You're team leader. Who will you take?"

"Me and Krishi are a team!" calls out Saeed at once, linking his arm with yours and pulling you close to him as if you are playing a game and not volunteering for a dangerous mission.

"Okay," Shivani agrees, and describes the assignment. "We need to figure out how the Narbolins are smuggling weapons in. You need to go out into the countryside. Whoever tried to poison the King had help getting into the castle. Our best guess is that one of the nobles may have been involved," Shivani continues. "The estate of the Baroness of Two Rivers is not far from here. She is having a big banquet tomorrow evening and most of the merchant nobles in the region will be there. We need you to infiltrate the manor and try to find out what is going on."

Go to section 49.

SECTION 49

First thing the next morning, you and Saeed are given two spirited ponies and provisions for the journey. Master Rabab, the master who teaches the classes on culture and language, accompanies you from the Farmhouse on her own mount, a dappled mare with a chestnut mane. She goes with you as far as the road to Ribbon Creek, the smaller of the Two Rivers.

"If you follow the creekside path," master Rabab says, "you will come to a small bridge. Cross to the other side, and the eastern road through the forest leads out to the bluff where the Baroness's manor overlooks the Bay of Albahr."

"What lies the other way?" you ask.

"That road exits the forest and leads back into the canyons," she says. "There's nothing that way but some folk who farm the cacti."

"You can farm cacti?" Saeed asks.

Rabab smiles. "Indeed," she says. "Some cacti can be cooked and eaten as vegetables, and the prickly pears fetch a pretty price."

You continue on your own, riding through the afternoon. Before long, you reach the bridge that Rabab mentioned. Your ponies' hooves clatter lightly on the wooden planks as you cross. Halfway across the bridge, you pause, looking down into the sparkling surface of Ribbon Creek, which is actually a small river despite its name.

"Where does this creek run?" you wonder aloud.

"All the way to Faldon River, I think," says Saeed, referring to the main river in the eastern part of Elaria, which empties into the Bay of Albahr.

You ride across the bridge and pause at the fork, looking first to the east, in the direction of the Baroness's estate, and then to the west.

"Krishi," says Saeed, "what are you thinking?"

"If the Narbolins are smuggling weapons into the countryside," you say, "wouldn't they use one of those hidden coves the Duchess hid in when she brought us here? It seems likely they would bring them in this way. Maybe one of those cactus farmers in the canyons knows something about it. It would be a simple trick to ferry the weapons down this river to the Faldon. I know we were supposed to go to the Baroness's house, but if the King is safe, then maybe we should take this chance to investigate the weapons shipments."

Saeed's eyes widen. "You might be right, Krishi! This could be our only chance to stop the weapons shipments at the source!"

If you decide to ride down into the canyon to investigate, turn to section 60.

If you stay on mission, go to the manor house in section 61.

SECTION 50

You approach the second door and are about to open it when you hear movements behind it.

"There's someone inside," you whisper to Etheldreda.

Who? she mouths back.

You turn back to the door and furrow your brow, reaching out with your mind, hoping you can recognize the thoughts of the people in the room. There's only one person inside. You need to be very subtle because sometimes a person can recognize that they are being read. You pull back and try to observe. Whoever is in the room is agitated. And familiar. You know this mind. But who—

And then it comes to you. You push the door open. At the far side of the room, near an opulent marble-tiled hallway that must lead to a bathing chamber, stands Arjun, the boy who Dev Acharya brought to the Citadel.

"You!"

He turns, alarmed.

Etheldreda's eyes go wide. "Archie!" She exclaims, and then covers her mouth with her hand. She drops into a deep curtsy. "Your Majesty," she says.

So *that's* what all of this has been about! Now you know the reason for Arjun's strange arrival and need for protection. Arjun was brought to the Citadel for protection because he is the King, and he is at the center of all of this. And now he is here.

Arjun—King Arjun, you correct yourself—strides toward you. "Dreda! How do you know Krishi? What is the meaning of this?" he asks imperiously.

"We hardly expected to find you here, Your Majesty," you say.

"Dev brought me to the Citadel to protect me from a plot against me, but then the Baroness sent her ships to tell me the coast was clear and that I must return at once. The Narbolins have asked me to sign a Writ of Accession."

"You can't, Your Majesty," Etheldreda begs.

"I don't have a choice," he says with a wan smile. "The council is divided on the issue, with the Countess and the Baroness supporting it actively. The Duc de Berry is pragmatic enough to side with whichever side is winning, and the Marquis de Bois—well, no one really knows what he wants. I don't have the support to stand against the Emperor on my own. Signing the document will be the best chance of avoiding full hostilities between our peoples."

"But Arjun—Your Majesty—"

He waves his hand to silence you. "There is no time left for discussion. We must proceed downstairs. When the Baroness told me that the Countess, the Duc, and the Marquis would all be here, I agreed to an impromptu meeting of the council to determine our course forward. Leave me be, please. I will join you in the reception hall when it is time."

You turn to Etheldreda. It sounds like you still have some time before the council meeting.

If you want to check out the baronial suite, go to section 51.

If you want to look into the old housekeeper's office, go to section 80.

SECTION 51

You open the heavy carved doors of the baronial suite. There's a small reception area with comfortable chairs and a table. The private room beyond is incredible. A great four-poster bed stands raised two steps up. Richly carved end tables flank either side. Somewhat beyond you can see the bathing chamber.

"How does the water come up from the ground?" you ask. "They didn't have anything like this at the Citadel! We had to go down into the caves to bathe in the salt pool from the sea!"

"Hydraulics," says Etheldreda matter-of-factly. "It's gardening technology. Should I ever become baroness again, I'll send engineers to the Citadel to teach you."

Quickly you split up. You start searching the reception area, but Etheldreda goes straight to the end table on the far side of the bed, just below a prismatic stained-glass window.

"My maedaw used to hide her most sensitive documents beneath a secret panel"—you hear a click as Etheldreda springs the panel—"and here they are," she drawls, drawing a fat packet of documents out.

You hurry over. She has a distressed look on her face as she scans the documents.

"Krishi, it's the Duke. The Duke of Kulsum. He's the one that inveigled the Duchess to attempt the poisoning of the King. It's all here in this letter. He's promising her access to the water-roads."

"Which he doesn't have any more," you say.

"Why's that?"

"His charts were stolen," you say, smirking.

"Krishi, this is what we need! We can have the Baroness arrested for treason and the council will just have to have a new election to elect another baroness."

"I'm not sure, Etheldreda," you say. "Maybe we should continue searching."

"There isn't time," she insists. "This is damning evidence!"

You agree that the evidence is important, but you still hear lively music below. Something tells you there is more upstairs you need to see.

"What if there is something else that could help us?" you say. "Why waste this chance to find everything we need?"

If you want to investigate the guest room, go to section 50.

If you think you have enough to confront the Baroness, go to section 58.

If you want to investigate the housekeeper's office, go to section 80.

SECTION 52

"Show me this ledger book," King Arjun says.

You hand over the book. He turns the pages, one after the other, his expression unreadable.

Etheldreda steps up next to him and points into the book. "Here, Your Majesty, are the names of ships. Here are the inventories of weapons they are bringing in."

"And?" Arjun says skeptically. "Where are these weapons going? For whom are they meant? This is a serious accusation you are making."

"Your Majesty," the Baroness croons superciliously. "All of this can be explained. I am an honest businesswoman, dealing in light arms for the militias of my fellow Albahri nobles. There is nothing underhanded happening here."

Arjun flicks past a few more pages and closes the book with a snap. "Dreda, I am sorry, but I am inclined to agree with the Baroness. This flimsy evidence shall not distract us from our business today. You have miscalculated. Away with you," he says, flicking his fingers in your direction.

Etheldreda's expression falls. Guards seize either arm. You scan the crowd quickly for Saeed but he's nowhere to be seen. You sigh in relief. At least there's a chance he got away and can get help. But for now, it's

THE END

SECTION 53

Arjun's expression changes instantly. Instead of polished disdain, he shows alarm.

"What?"

"Here they are, Your Majesty," says Etheldreda, drawing the packet of letters from a pocket in her uniform.

You are watching the Countess's face carefully. From pure terror, she quickly shifts to a canny expression. "Your Majesty," she says, with practiced shock. "Could this be true?"

"It appears so," Arjun says softly, flipping through the letters. "Lowelia, how could you?"

The Baroness backs up, terror in her eyes. Her own guards step closer on either side to flank her. "Protect your Baroness, Dannel!" she snaps at the younger guard.

"Eh," says Dannel languidly, scratching at his beard. "We don't work for you, my lady, but the Barony itself. If you're in collusion against the King, we have to wait for the council's word."

"And you, Duc de Berry," the Baroness says in alarm. "What say you?"

"We must look at all the evidence," says the Duc de Berry sententiously. "We must convene the entire Guild of Merchants to discuss what is to be done."

"There's no time for that," the Countess says. "The proof is there in the King's hands!"

She pivots quickly, you think to yourself. *Best keep our eyes on that one!*

"Well," says King Arjun, turning to the elderly man in the corner of the room, absently plucking lyre strings. "Marquis de Bois, it appears that the tie breaking vote is yours. The Baroness and I are the aggrieved parties. You must determine whether we take this to the Guild of Merchants or whether we must take immediate action of a more . . . decisive manner."

The Baroness gulps.

If you have a silver acorn in your pocket, go to section 54.

If you have a golden acorn in your pocket, go to section 59.

SECTION 54

"**O**h, but first, my Lord," you say, stepping forward and holding out the acorn, "a song."

The Marquis's face lights up with pleasure. He picks up the lyre and a plectrum and begins plucking out a discordant but weirdly beautiful tune.

"I was but a wee boy when I first heard this song from my maemaw," he says wistfully, his eyes rolling back as he plays. And then he begins singing:

> *Oh little lad who wandered*
> *through the darkened wood,*
> *how will maemaw find you*
> *if under the moons you hid?*
>
> *Only if you act like the moons*
> *and let your face shine bright*
> *will your maemaw find you*
> *by the moons' silver light!*

As the notes die away, the room is silent.

"Do as you must, King Arjun," says the Marquis simply. "But spare Lowelia her life. She at least threw a very nice party." He smiles and replaces the lyre.

In the hush that follows, Arjun smiles. "My lord, the Marquis de Bois. You are as wise a man as ever spoke in council," he says. He turns back to the Baroness and the others and draws himself up. Even though he is only your age, he is still taller than both the Baroness and the Duc de Berry. "You have dishonored your office, Baroness Lowelia. I remove you from this station of honor." He turns to look at the Duc.

The Duc inclines his head. "It is your body that has been insulted, Your Majesty, and your right to pass the judgment."

"Your Majesty," you interject, "Etheldreda here is the granddaughter of the old Baroness, and has been living and working here this entire time. She can step in and take on the responsibilities of the Baroness with no delay."

Arjun looks at you, bemused, and then looks back at the Marquis de Bois. "What do you say to this solution, Your Grace?"

The Marquis blinks, unaccustomed, perhaps, to being taken so seriously. "The young lass is quiet and graceful, Your Majesty. I knew her maedaw well."

"Well then," says Arjun. "It is settled. Etheldreda—Baroness Etheldreda—as well as the Countess and the Duc, please accompany me upstairs to my quarters where I will draw up the proclamation."

"Your Majesty," says Etheldreda firmly, "I shall take this great honor only under one condition."

Arjun's eyebrow raises in surprise.

"I'll have no truck with the Narbolins. I'll not support you signing any writ or making any concession to them."

Arjun looks from her to the Duc. The Duc slowly, reluctantly nods. "You have my support, Your Majesty, if you want to stand up to the Emperor."

"Then stand up we shall," says Arjun with determination. "Krishi, come. You must witness the signing and investiture of our newest Baroness!"

THE END

SECTION 55

"My lord," you say, bowing your head, "a dance is freely given, especially to one who takes such pleasure in it. But I have heard it said you offer a tremendous gift of your own."

The Marquis breaks out into a great smile.

"It would be more than rich payment were you to sing again tonight," you conclude genuinely.

He smiles and takes your hands in his. "I will gladly sing for you tonight or any other night," the Marquis promises, his kindly face crinkling with delight. "And here," he places a beautifully fashioned silver acorn in your palm, "is the token for you to redeem in exchange for my voice. Present the acorn and I will sing."

Go to section 57.

SECTION 56

"**M**y lord," you say, "I am here with a friend, Etheldreda. She once lived in this house."

"Did she?" the Marquis asks, but you can tell he is only being polite.

"She seeks audiences to talk about the future of the Barony."

"Ah, well," the Marquis says, looking about, distracted. "Perhaps we can talk later."

"I was hoping to introduce you," you say urgently.

"My friend," he says then, "since I was elected to the council—I can't imagine why they elected me really—people have been bringing their suits to me night and day. It's quite exhausting, I promise you. If you will excuse me, I want to find some refreshment. Here is my token, a golden acorn."

"A golden acorn, my lord?"

"If you find me later, present it, and I shall introduce you to my attendant and perhaps a meeting can be facilitated. Ah, Countess!" He leaves you standing in the middle of the room and bustles off into the crowd.

Go to section 79.

SECTION 57

You hurry into the foyer. There's no sight of Zubaydah, but Etheldreda stands there.

"Come on, Krishi! I got distracted by a group of nobles who wanted me to fetch drinks for them! We're nearly out of time!"

Go to section 79.

SECTION 58

You and Etheldreda go downstairs and enter the reception hall. The Baroness and the Duc de Berry have returned from the garden.

"Where have you been?" Saeed demands, scurrying up to you, an empty tray under his arm. "I had to keep Javid really busy so he didn't notice you were gone!"

You wave Saeed to silence, and there is a sudden commotion at the entrance. The crowd of nobles parts. Striding into the room, dressed in a richly embroidered coat of blue silk, is Arjun.

"Your Majesty," purrs the Baroness, curtsying deeply as all those around her repeat the moment.

"Rise, my friends. I have come back to Albahr from across the sea," he says.

"Your Majesty," says the Countess in a somewhat snarky tone, "you are not meant to leave the territory of Albahr."

"There were some concerns for my safety, Your Grace," he says. "Which have passed."

"It's time, then," says the Duc de Berry, "to address the question of signing the Writ of Accession. In the best interests of the security of Albahr—"

"Wait!" you cry out. Everyone's eyes turn to you. Arjun's gaze looks murderous.

"Yes?" he says icily.

"Your Majesty, I believe signing the Writ would be hasty. We have evidence of nefarious action!"

"And this is? Make it brief, friend. My patience is thin."

If you say, "We have a ledger book showing the Baroness has been involved in smuggling weapons in to Albahr!," go to section 52.

If you say, "We have letters between the Baroness and the Duke of Kulsum proving that they were the ones plotting to poison you!," go to section 53.

SECTION 59

The Marquis turns from the lyre he was strumming. "Oh, Your Majesty, you know I haven't much of a head for matters of politics like this."

"We will take it to the Guild of Merchants then," Arjun says reluctantly.

"You cannot mean to leave this woman in charge of the Barony until then," the Countess snaps.

She's alarmed, you think. There must be something in the documents to incriminate her as well. Still, the primary goal is to ensure Etheldreda becomes the next Baroness.

"Might I suggest a solution, Your Majesty," you say.

He turns to you, his face reflecting his interest. "Go on."

"Etheldreda was the granddaughter of the old Baroness. She knows the land better than anyone else. She can run things here while you go to the Guild of Merchants and resolve things with the Baroness."

"Fair enough," says Arjun. "Take the Baroness to her quarters," he instructs the guards, "and confine her there. We leave for Albahr in the morning."

The guards remove the sullen Baroness. The other guests begin to disperse, heading for the cloakroom. Some who came from afar are shown to guest quarters by the suddenly obsequious Javid.

Saeed appears beside you, clapping his hands. You and he hug Etheldreda from both sides.

"You did it!" Saeed cries. "You're a baroness!"

"Not a baroness yet," she says. "Just acting as one. Time will tell. Listen, did you get a look at the Countess?"

"Something fishy is going on there," you agree.

"I will," you hear Arjun saying then. Looking across the room, you see he is deep in conversation with the Duc de Berry. "Immediately upon my return to Albahr, I shall sign the Writ. Do not worry, Your Grace, we will avoid military conflict with the Narbolins."

"Ugh," says Etheldreda. "A treacherous Countess, a King about to sign the Writ of Accession, and fields full of land underproducing."

"And don't forget that you have to remove all that gold paint from the front of the house," says Saeed in a serious tone, but with a gleam in his eyes.

"Who knew the burdens of leadership could be so alarming and so ordinary at the same time?"

"There's a lot of work to do," you agree, "but every noble is assigned Whisperers if they ask. If you request it, I will stay here and help. We'll find solutions to all of these problems."

"Yes," says Etheldreda, covering your hand with hers. "I would like that, my friend. There is much work to do."

THE END

SECTION 60

You follow the path along the creek, then through the forest. Slowly, as you travel, the forest leads into the ridges and valleys of the canyons. The sky darkens as the tree cover grows thicker. After a time you come to a path leading into one of the canyons.

You turn your ponies down the path back into the sun and travel between the dwindling trees into the deserted canyon, the cacti thick on either side of the path, prickly pears shining bright pink among the perfusion of wicked-looking needles.

After a time, you see a postern, weathered with age. The main path continues down the cactus-lined cavern, but among sage and other bushes, another cart track leads past the postern into a vale. You pause, considering your next move, when a figure steps out of the bushes around the ruined structure and into the path. It is a child, perhaps seven or eight years old, not much smaller than Saeed, with crudely cut sandy-brown hair.

"Who are you?" the child asks.

"Who are you?" you ask in return.

"I'm Max," the child says. "Are you the workers promised to come and help us pick the pears?"

"We are," you say smoothly, reaching as delicately as you can into the child's mind to find the names of the workers the family is expecting. "My name is Nakul and this is Sahadev."

Max blinks. "If you say so."

Saeed's gaze flicks over to you. "Who else would we be?" he asks the child carefully.

Max turns to look straight at you, and you have an odd feeling.

"If I wanted to guess," says Max then, "I'd say your name is not Nakul, but I think there's a 'K' in it. And your name," he turns to Saeed, "does actually sound like Sahadev, but that's not really it."

You stop your mouth from falling open, but you look at Saeed in alarm. Max has the talent to be a Whisperer, you realize. He is around the same age you were when Chandh Sahib came to your home to recruit you.

Max shrugs his shoulders. "But what do I know?" he says carelessly. "My daw says I shouldn't make stories up and my maw says it is rude to look inside people's heads without their permission. Which you can never really get, can you? Because who thinks you can actually look inside someone's head?"

"Who indeed?" you say, trying not to laugh. "We would like to meet your parents, though."

Max gestures you over and heads down the path. You dismount and walk your ponies along behind him.

About a hundred feet down from the main path, the cart track opens into clear ground about twenty yards across. There is a dwelling to your left, at the far end, nestled against the base of the canyon slope. You can see an adjacent shed without a front, where various tools are stored, and off to the right, across the grounds, are the stables.

A woman wearing a long skirt and apron comes out of the cabin and spots you.

"Mags!" she calls in a voice inflected with an accent you haven't heard since your childhood in the farmlands.

"Maw," yells Max. "It's Max! *Max!*" He turns to you, sullen, and says to you, as if he's reminding you, "It's *Max.*"

The woman waves you over. "Max," she says, emphasizing the name, "will you take their ponies to the stable?"

Max takes the reins to your mounts and says, "Maw, these are Nakul and Sahadev. They come to help us pick the pears."

"Oh, thank God," the woman says. "Harvesting has been very difficult this year; there's so much more work. I'm Meghan. My husband Rubio is out in the thatch, picking pears. He'll be back soon. But in the meantime, let me show you the place you'll be staying."

As she leads you into the cabin, you ask, "Why has the work been more difficult this year?"

"Oh," she says, waving a hand in the air, "there's always so much to do on a farm."

You exchange a quick glance with Saeed. You try to project his way, *Are you thinking what I'm thinking?* Saeed gives an imperceptible nod.

The main door leads right into the large, well-lit kitchen. Straight ahead is a large pantry. Off to the right, the kitchen stretches quite a ways. On the wall next to the pantry is a large stone hearth, at the far end are large wooden cupboards, padlocked shut, and to your right is a counter with two large basins and water pumps. The window faces the yard.

"Rubio is quite an engineer," Meghan says, gesturing to the pumps. "He said he could bring the well water inside the house and sure enough he did it."

"About Max," you say tentatively. "There's something about him—"

"Oh, Max," she says with a dismissive smile, as she leads you down the long hallway to the left. "Max says that when he was inside me he was a boy but when he came out he came out as a girl so we called him Maggie, but now that he remembers he is a boy we are to call him Max." She ducks her head, smiling. "Rubio and Max's brother Tommy always remember, but me, I forget sometimes."

You smile kindly at Meghan. She seems openhearted, and to care deeply for her family. *Trying to bring up Whisperers right now wouldn't be right*, you think.

You reach the end of the hallway, where there is a room with several bunks. "And here we are," she says, brushing a stray lock of hair behind her ears. "You must want to rest! You've had a long journey here. Rubio will be back for the evening meal. He can explain everything to you then." She leaves, pulling the door shut behind her.

"Okay," you say slowly. "What is she not telling us?"

"Do you think she knows Max can read people's minds?"

"I'm not sure," you say. "Maybe he thinks he's just playing a game. Or maybe she knows about the Whisperers."

"The only way she," Saeed gestures in the direction of the

kitchen, "could know about the Whisperers is if she used to be one."

"My ma was a Whisperer," you say. "Maybe Meghan used to be one too. But whatever is going on, there has to be a reason why they are taking on extra help."

Beyond the door, you hear the clattering of cart wheels and a man's voice shouting greetings. You and Saeed leave your packs in the room and go down the hallway and back into the kitchen. Meghan is at the large cabinets at the far end of the room. A small man with red curly hair has come in along with a boy your age not much smaller than the man.

"Ah, Rubio, Tommy," says Meghan, closing the cabinet doors and locking a heavy padlock. "These are our helpers, Nakul and Sahadev. They've come to help with the harvest."

"All the harvest?" asks a young man who has come in behind them. He is tall and well-built, and you notice immediately that though he is unshaven and is dressed in the same type of rough garments that Rubio and Tommy are wearing, his clothes, hair, and hands are clean, while Rubio and Tommy are covered in brambles and dirt. He has not been among the cactus thickets. *This man is not a farmer*, you think.

"Oh no, Doron," Rubio says quickly, "just with the cacti!" He looks worried.

"All right then," Doron says, going back out into the grounds, where four or five other young men lounge around a crate which has been set up as a table. They are playing some kind of card game and taking swigs out of a bottle of amber liquid.

Rubio exhales a shuddering breath, looking over at you. "I'm sorry about that. There are a lot of different things that happen on a farm. If you'll excuse me, I will wash up before dinner. Come, Tommy." The two of them disappear down the hallway.

Meghan looks over at you, wringing her hands. When she speaks, you can tell she is distracted.

"Well, dinner is already prepared, so I will go and check on Max and feed the chickens. Will you two be all right on your own?"

You nod, smiling, and Meghan excuses herself and disappears out the back entrance of the kitchen, into the small alley abutting the canyon wall that leads out to the yard.

"Quick," you say to Saeed, "we have a little time before dinner. Should we sit down with Doron's men and try to learn more about why they're here?"

"I'm more curious about what's inside this house," Saeed says. "What was in that cabinet she locked up? That was no ordinary lock."

If you join the men in the yard and try to figure out what is going on, go to section 62.

If you want to check out the cabinet that Meghan locked, go to section 63.

SECTION 61

"Let's stick with the plan," you announce. "The manor house is where we were sent and that's where we stand the best chance of success."

The road you are following eventually exits the forest. It forks, one branch leading off to the northeast and widening on its way to the city of Albahr, the other leading up along the bluffs that overlook the Blue Sea. Gazing across the expanse, you wonder what is happening at the Citadel, whether Sandhya and the others are faring well. There's no time for dreaming, though, because soon you come to the string of manors that overlook the sea to the west of the great Bay of Albahr where the city and its famous harbors sit.

Each manor belongs to one of the merchant lords of the Two Rivers district. At the crest of the bluff on the westernmost point of the bay, the road ends at the palatial home of Lowelia, the Baroness of Two Rivers.

You blink at the gaudy façade of the manor. It's possible the house once looked graceful in the pink granite that this part of

Elaria is so known for, but someone—the Baroness, likely—has commissioned artisans to paint swirling gold leaves along the entire surface of the manor. The pillars in front are painted solid in the same material. As you ride up the wide drive, you see the pillars have also been speckled with some kind of small stone, so they seem to shimmer and sparkle in the sunlight.

"Ghastly," you say, and Saeed nods his fervent agreement.

You ride past the house to the rear where the stables—and the servants' entrances—typically are. You pass the house garden. A number of workers are bent at their work, troweling and weeding and planting, talking and laughing as they work. One, a tall girl with tawny braids nearly as long as Shivani's, stands and wipes sweat off her forehead with one arm. She catches your eye and waves, nodding a greeting.

You come to the rear of the manor, where several small houses sit—one a carriage house for the horses, the others no doubt servants' quarters or guesthouses.

"New servants come to work the banquet?" bawls out a short, balding man on the steps.

"Sir, we came as quick as we were called," you say, nodding.

"Fine. We can use the help. I'm Javid, the castellan. Pitch your horses in the rear stables. I'll give you tools and you can go on to the gardens."

Go to section 67.

SECTION 62

"Let's see if we can learn who those men are and what they are up to," you say to Saeed.

When you pass through the kitchen, Meghan is nowhere to be seen. A pot is bubbling on the hearth and you hear Meghan in the small alley that runs between the back of the house and the steep canyon wall. Out in the yard, the men continue to play their card game and pass the open bottle, their voices growing louder and more aggressive.

"Come on," you tell Saeed, "this is our chance."

You stroll out into the yard, willing yourself to forget that you have a mission. You try to focus on acting like you're here to have a good time with the men. If you really were a farm laborer who had traveled all day to get here, that's what you would want to do, you remind yourself.

"Room for two more in the game, boys?" you call out cheerily.

"For sure, governor," says a lad who couldn't be more than sixteen. He's the youngest in the group and has an eager smile. "I'm Casey," he says. "And this is my bruv, Finnegan."

"It's Finn," says the other boy, who couldn't look more different from Casey. Finn is lanky where Casey is stout, his hair is brown and straight while Casey has red curls, and he's got big jug-ears and a long nose, while Casey has a little button nose with freckles dusted across it.

"We're twins, if you'd believe it," announced Casey. "Swear to me maw, we are!"

Doron, the man you saw with Rubio, says, "Aye, they are. I can vouch for them." He takes a pull from the bottle. "I'm Doron," he says. "And these are Alec and Caleb," he gestures to the other two men, older, a little surlier than Casey and Finnegan. Both men grunt hellos but are focused on the bottle Doron has passed them.

"Have a pull, lads?" asks Caleb, once he's sipped from the bottle.

"Not for me, thanks," you say. "It's been a long day on the road. If I have some, I'll abed before I can eat some of Meghan's stew and play some cards with you lot!"

"That's a lad," says Doron enthusiastically, slapping you on the back. "Your friend here looks a little young to be playing cards with the big boys, though." He casts a critical eye over Saeed, who—though he is the same age as you—is at least six inches shorter and skinny enough to be mistaken for a younger boy.

You laugh. "That he is," you say, trying to imitate the bluff speech of the men. *Look for Max,* you think toward Saeed. *Whatever happens next, we need to keep tabs on him.*

Saeed laughs nervously too. "Yeah, I think I'll just—" and he begins edging away from the men toward the stable where Max's brother and father are unhitching their horses.

"All right, boys, everyone in the crew knows this game called Wonder. I assume you know it too, since you've been working the farm circuit," Doron says to you offhandedly.

"Sure I do," you say slowly. "Wonder."

Doron deals out three cards to each man, and then puts the remainder of the cards in four little piles between you. He taps the top of each small deck in succession, announcing, "Flowers, jewels, birds, clouds."

You pick up your cards. You have a jasmine vine, a humming-bird, and a card that shows a blue sky striped by wispy white clouds.

Alec puts down a card bearing daffodils.

"Oh buddy," commiserates Caleb, putting down a white rose. Alec clucks.

Finn blows through his teeth in frustration and puts down a card with garnet crystals, then looks over to his brother.

Casey smiles slyly and places down a red rose. The other men cry out. "Sorry, friend," says Casey apologetically. You pause, looking down at your cards.

"It's your move," says Doron. "Taker of the first trick wins the right to call the trump suit."

You're guessing by the men's reactions that your jasmine flower will not beat Casey's rose.

If you play the card with the clouds, go to section 64.

If you play the card with the hummingbird, go to section 65.

SECTION 63

"The cupboard," you say. "They obviously don't want us to see what's inside these cupboards."

"Can you look inside with magic?" Saeed asks, making a mysterious little gesture with his fingers.

You grimace. "I don't think so. I think we're going to have to do it the old-fashioned way and pick these locks. Do you want to be lookout?"

"Let me try the padlock," Saeed insists, hopping up and down, clasping his hands together, pleading. "You be lookout."

If you let Saeed try to pick the lock, go to section 69.

If you insist Saeed be lookout, go to section 70.

SECTION 64

You calmly lay down the card with the clouds, and Casey groans.

"Why did you throw out your highest card on the first round?" Finn admonishes as Casey buries his face in his hands. "This guy doesn't understand basic strategy," Finn announces to the table.

You sweep the cards in a pile toward you. "Sorry, boys," you say, "it's newcomer's luck."

Everyone laughs and the bottle gets passed again. You keep your eyes sharp on the cards and by the time the fourth round arrives and a new set of three cards is being dealt, you are tied with Finn, who has cannily won two rounds himself.

"Let me have a little break," begs Casey. "I got to relieve myself before Meghan serves the grub!" He jumps up and makes for the outhouse, down a little path into the woods.

"You can handle your cards," says Doron, "and you know enough to pass on some of this fire-brew these boys call a drink, so it may happen I could have work for you."

"Work?" you ask. "What kind of work?"

"Look," says Doron, leaning forward to speak to you in confidence. "We're all honest men here, honest countrymen of Two Rivers. We're beholden to Albahr by compact and law, but we mostly want to live our own lives and not always be sending a cut of everything we earn and grow off to fatten the cats in the capital."

"I'm listening," you say.

"So it happens that we have a chance to do a good deed for ourselves and it don't cost us a thing. The Narbolins want the city. Happen if they get it, they'll cut us loose. Least that's what was promised. All we have to do is this. The sailors bring weapons into the cove and down the canyon paths. They're stored here and then when we get the message, we pack the lot up and take it inland to the men who are waiting for it."

"Where did they come from?"

"They came in through Albahr. See how neat it is? The King of Albahr won't ever know there's an army landing because he doesn't know how to look for it."

"What would I do?" you ask.

"Well, lad, the message came in. We send you off with Casey and Finnegan to deliver the weapons, while Alec and Caleb and I stay here waiting for the next shipment; otherwise, if you're not in the mood for traveling, you lot stay here and we'll take the weapons on."

Just then Saeed returns. Max is with him.

"Your friend will have to stay here either way," says Doron. "Dangerous mission is no place for a little niblet."

If you agree to deliver the weapons, go to section 45.

If you think it is better to stay with Saeed, Max, and the farmers, go to section 107.

SECTION 65

You lay down the hummingbird and Casey groans.

"Whoa, you're throwing your best cards away for nothing!" he exclaims. "Why'd you do that?"

Doron's expression changes to one of disgust as he lays down a card bearing a pigeon, and Casey sweeps the cards into a small pile in front of him.

"Fine, as long as you're throwing away your best birds," says Casey, laying down a card showing a peregrine falcon. "Can't beat that now, I'd wager."

The next two rounds go quickly, but Doron doesn't say anything more to you. After the third card is played, he claps his hands and stands up. "All right, gents," he announces, "the game is over. Chores to finish before Meghan serves dinner. Casey, you check on the horses for the night journey. You and Finn will get on to Albahr before nightfall."

"Aw, Doron, really? Meghan's made cornbread tonight!"

Doron laughs shortly. "It's Albahr for you 'n' Finn tonight, me lad. Alec and Caleb will stay here at the farm to keep an eye on things and I've got a hankering to look at the ocean. Full moons tonight," he says, meaningfully.

Grumbling, Casey and Finn disappear into the house, while Alec and Caleb start saddling up the horses. Doron sets the deck of cards down in the middle of the box. "Good game," he says shortly, and then he too goes off toward the stables, leaving you alone in the yard.

Hey Krishi, you hear, as if someone's speaking right in your ear, and you spin around. Saeed and Max are huddled by the side of the house. Saeed gestures you toward them with a crook of his finger. You look to see you aren't being watched and steal over to where they hide.

"What's going on?" you say in a low tone.

"Max is a Whisperer," says Saeed, eyes bright with excitement.

"Not a Whisperer yet," you correct, "but you have talent, Max. How long have you been able to hear in people's minds? And speak into them?"

Max shrugs. "I don't remember. But it is definitely after I stopped being Mags and started being Max."

You look over at Saeed. "Could that have something to do with it?"

Saeed shrugs. "They pick younger kids than Max to come to the Citadel. They pick up who has talent somehow."

"But not every young student becomes a Whisperer," you remind Saeed. Some of the youngest students go away to other schools and never advance in their studies the way you, Saeed, and Zara did.

"Either way," says Saeed, "one of the first Rumors of

Whispering is that when you find someone with the talent, you are supposed to bring them in."

"Bring me 'in'?" demands Max. "What does that mean?"

"The talents—hearing people's minds, being able to access magical objects, other things Whisperers can do—they're too important to be left alone. When a Whisperer comes across someone with potential, we're required to bring them to a senior master to assess. Then you either become a student of the Whisperer or—"

"Or what?" Max asks crossly.

"Or . . . I don't really know. I never heard of someone who didn't want to join up."

"Well, I don't," Max declares stoutly. "This is my home. This is my family. You can see they're in trouble. We have to stay."

"It's not that simple," Saeed says. "We are bound by this rule, Max. If we stay and those men get on to us, there's no telling what kind of trouble we'd be in, especially if they find out we're Whisperers."

"First we take care of my family. Then I'll think about going with you," Max says.

If you insist Max leave the farm with you and Saeed, go to section 68.

If you agree to stay with Max on the farm, go to section 110.

SECTION 66

You ou reach down and open the ice chest. Right in the front sits a dish of gleaming pale-green fruit with a dark thin rind, already sliced. It seems to match the drink, so you spear them and drop one slice along the top of each drink. The slice floats, almost covering the surface of the glass. To sip the drink, you would have to sip along the surface of the fruit, which likely gives it a lovely little kick of flavor.

Proud of yourself, you balance the tray and head through one of the doors that a helpful kitchen worker holds open for you.

The dining hall is full of finely dressed people. The long table that had been set for the first meal has been taken to the side of the room opposite the wide window facing the sea. The surface of the table is covered with fruit, meats, and other delicacies.

You approach a group of nobles of which the Baroness is part.

"My lords," you say, bowing slightly and presenting the tray.

"What is the meaning of this?" demands the Baroness, an imperious-looking woman in a red dress woven through with gold threads.

"Madam, your drinks," you say, getting nervous.

"Garnished with the fruit I slice for my cats to lick? Javid!" The Baroness turns and gestures perfunctorily for the castellan. "You choose my staff, do you not? How do you explain this?" She stabs her finger at you.

Javid's expression is as dark as a thundercloud. "Into the kitchen!" he shouts.

You can't blow your cover so you bow your head ashamedly and follow him.

Javid puts you on potato-peeling duty in the pantry closet for the rest of the party. You don't know if they're even serving potatoes, but you're sure he wants to keep you out of sight until he can deal with you.

You have no way of knowing whether Etheldreda or Saeed was successful, but you know you have failed.

THE END

SECTION 67

fter you have handed the reins of your horses over to the stable girl, Javid hands you a trowel and Saeed a straw basket.

"The garden boss will tell you what to do," he says. "Ask for Margalit."

You and Saeed walk down the path to the house garden. The garden is surrounded by a low wall and there are more than a dozen long rows of vegetables, including spinach, cabbage, squash, and others you don't recognize. At one end of the garden are rows of beautifully colored flowers, and at the other end you see a watermelon patch and a row of neatly trimmed, lushly producing fruit trees.

Margalit, the boss, is a stout woman, built like a warrior and with a voice like a squadron of trumpets.

"Scrubs!" she shouts in your direction. "Work with Dreda harvesting the greens!" She gestures you toward the tall girl you'd seen earlier.

You approach, smiling. She smiles back at you, and instantly you like her. "It's Etheldreda," she calls out to Margalit.

"Oh, all right, my lady," the boss says with a malicious smile. "Of course, Your Grace."

Etheldreda flushes darkly and turns back to you. "She knows just how to stick it to me," she says. "She was my governess when I was a little lassie and she loves that I'm her employee now."

"Your governess?" you ask, dropping down to your knees beside her.

"My maedaw was actually the Baroness in her day, but neither my daw nor my maw had any interest in business and trade at all, so when it came time for the merchant lords to choose the next baroness, they chose Lady Lowelia," Etheldreda explains while you work. "My daw and maw moved to Albahr and make a living as tailors. My daw actually sews really well. He makes all the nobles' fineries. My maw can't sew but she draws the pictures that my daw uses to make the dresses. I just couldn't leave here. I love it too much. Lady Lowelia let me stay."

"Why did you choose to work in the fields then?"

"I love this land, even the dirt it is made of. Especially the dirt it is made of," she confesses with a smile on her face.

You bend to the work. Etheldreda shows you how to select the leaves to pluck, and Saeed holds out the basket for you both to gather them. The sun is hot upon you, but you enjoy the quiet, repetitive labor. Its predictable nature is soothing.

"I know what your amulet means," Etheldreda says casually, and you quickly tuck it back under your shirt from where it came free and dangled in her view while you worked.

"And what do you think it means?" you ask her carefully, intensely aware that even the existence of the Whisperers is meant to be kept secret.

"From when my maedaw was Baroness. I saw people with that amulet. I know who you are. I know you can be trusted."

You decide there is no point in lying to her, but you also know you must be careful.

"What do you wish to trust me with?" you ask, keeping your eyes on the plants lest Margalit see you all slacking off in your work.

"Lady Lowelia is in over her head," says Etheldreda, her brow furrowing, keeping her eyes on the greens, same as you. "She's made a deal with the Duke of Kulsum to help the Narbolins. She's going to allow him into Two Rivers territorial waters so the navy of Kulsum can blockade Albahr once the Emperor makes his move."

"And how do you know this?"

"The servants hear talk. I've heard it too. But I don't have evidence."

"And when is it supposed to happen?" you ask, alarmed.

"Any time now," she confesses. "I was planning on acting tomorrow at the party. Enough of the merchant lords will be in attendance. We might have a chance to expose her plan and get her deposed as Baroness."

Saeed whistles.

"We were sent to find evidence of who it was that was conspiring with the Narbolins," you reveal. "Someone got them access to the palace for the attempt on the King's life. If it was the Duke, we need to know, but if it was the Baroness then it's even more important that you succeed."

"Maybe they were in it together," says Etheldreda.

"We can help each other," you determine. "What's your plan?"

"We sneak into the house tonight while everyone sleeps. I'm sure there's proof of her dealings with the Duke in the chest in her office."

"That sounds risky," Saeed says. "You don't know what kind of security she has."

"I know that house," Etheldreda avers. "And I know the staff. They'll help us."

"I don't know," Saeed says. "Wouldn't it be better to wait until the party is underway tomorrow? We could use that as a cover to search the house, plus that's when you have to put your plan into action anyhow."

If you think you Saeed's plan of waiting is better, go to section 71.

If you want to go with Etheldreda's idea and strike tonight, go to section 72.

SECTION 68

"Max," you say, crouching a little to look into his eyes, "listen to me. It's not safe. They're three grown men, and we have to protect your maw and daw too. If we stay and they figure out we're Whisperers, we're in big trouble. Doron already doesn't trust us. It's better for everyone if we sneak out tonight. We'll be halfway to the Farmhouse before they figure out we're gone."

Max looks at you a minute, and then nods. "Okay, Krishi."

Before long, Meghan rings the bell for supper. Casey and Finn accept parcels of dried meat and cheese that Meghan has packed for them and get underway, Casey driving the cart and Finn on horseback. You watch as the cart, laden with cargo, trundles out of the gate and down the cart path to the main road.

You all eat, more or less in silence, while Doron and Rubio make small talk about the harvest and the weather.

Later, after helping to clear the table, you, Max, and Saeed huddle in your room at the far end of the hallway.

"All right, you two, I will wait exactly one hour after lights out and then we meet in the yard. Doron said there is a full moon tonight so there'll be enough light to follow the trail to the forest. We can't risk making any noise by taking the horses, so we'll be on foot. If we make good time and move through the night, we'll make it to the Farmhouse before dawn."

"But there's not a full moon tonight," Max says. "The biggest moon is only about three quarters. Not sure why Doron wouldn't know that."

"It's a signal," says Saeed, snapping his fingers. "Something's happening tonight at the cove."

You nod.

"The shipment's probably coming in. If only there were a way to signal the Duchess," you say.

"Couldn't you just . . . ?" Max makes a kind of mystical twirl near his temple.

"It doesn't really work that way," you say. "Imagine if you were trying to call out to someone in a crowded stadium. You can still do it, but you kind of have to know where they are, right? And then you call out in their direction?"

Max nods, deflated.

Saeed says, "Maybe we could figure something else out? It's a risk."

You suppose you could follow Doron and see if an opportunity presents itself. But you worry that may be unsafe, especially for Max.

If you think it is better to go straight back to the Farmhouse, go to section 108.

If you want to follow Doron on the canyon trails, go to section 109.

SECTION 69

"**Y**ou better pick the lock, Saeed," you say, and Saeed jumps up and down, clapping his hands for a moment. You shoot him a look and he settles down, rubbing his hands together and flexing his fingers.

"Step back, step back," he says, pulling the hairpin out of his bound hair. "A master is working."

You head over to the counter and peer out the window. The men are still at their game. Behind you, you hear a click. Turning, you see that Saeed has popped the padlock open and is sliding it out of the lock. He opens the cupboard door and whistles.

The cupboard is full of weapons—swords, spears, axes. The Narbolins are smuggling weapons into the countryside.

"Whoa," you say, coming over to look.

"All the men coming in," says Saeed, "all the merchants. The Narbolins will get these weapons to them and—"

"They'll have an army," you say. "The war will be over before it starts."

"Krishi, we gotta do something. Now."

If you try to sneak out now before anyone notices, go to section 103.

If you want to stay to find out more, go to section 104.

SECTION 70

"**I** don't think it's a good idea, Saeed," you say. "You have better eyes anyhow, just keep a watch on the soldiers."

Saeed huffs in frustration, but goes over to the counter where the basins are. He ducks down so he can peep over the counter out the window to the yard, where the men are playing cards.

You turn back to the cabinet, looking around for an implement to try to pop the lock. You remember your hairpin, pull it out, and insert the needle end into the first big padlock. You jiggle it, trying to hear the tumblers. It's harder than you thought!

"Did you get it yet?" Saeed hisses, looking back toward you.

"No! Stop bugging me!" you say.

Suddenly you hear a clatter behind you. You and Saeed both whirl in the direction of the back door. Meghan stands there, the bucket she was carrying fallen to the ground at her feet.

"What on earth are you doing?" she says with shock.

You lift your finger to your lips, trying to quiet her down, but it is too late. The men from the yard have rushed in at the sound in the kitchen.

"Well, well," drawls Doron, his expression menacing. "What do we have here?"

"Thieves!" calls Rubio from the hallway, where he stands, his sons Max and Tommy peeking out from behind him. "They were trying to break in and steal food!" You meet Max's eyes. He looks back at you, unblinking. He knows.

"I do not think so," Doron drawls. "I think we have a more serious situation here." He draws a wicked-looking knife from a sheath at his belt.

"It's true," Max pipes up. "I heard them talking about how hungry they were, how they wanted to steal some food to put in their packs."

Doron pauses. He puts his knife away. "All right. But you've got thieves on your hands, farmer. What do you do with thieves?" he asks Rubio.

Rubio swallows. "Git!" he says to you then, harshly. "Get out of here and don't come back! Get their things!" he orders Max.

Meghan stands there, stock still, looking down at the floor as Max brings you and Saeed your things.

"I'll get your ponies," Max tells you, and heads off.

"All right, friends," drawls Doron. "Time for you to head out. And don't let me catch you hanging around. And you," he turns to Rubio, "no more outside help, old man. Get me?"

You and Saeed back out of the kitchen. Rubio keeps his frightened eyes on you, while Meghan is still staring at the floor.

You and Saeed mount your ponies without a word and ride off into the night. You have to make it back to the Farmhouse to report, but you know you failed this mission. The men are now alert and the family is in more danger than before. You hope that Shivani will be able to figure out how to clean up your mess.

THE END

SECTION 71

"$\mathcal{I}$ know it might not seem logical," you say to Etheldreda, "but it will actually be safer during the day. It doesn't matter how much you think you know the house, things might have changed. Plus, any sound we make will be magnified and anyone who sees us will know we're up to mischief. If we mix and mingle with the other servants during the day, we'll be hiding in plain sight."

"It'll be safer," Saeed assures her.

She's not happy about it but she agrees to go along with you. You focus on the gardening work for the rest of the day, and when, at the evening meal for the field-workers, Javid approaches and asks for volunteers to work in the house the next day, you, Saeed, and Etheldreda raise your hands along with several others. If he is surprised that Etheldreda is volunteering to work as a servant in a house her family used to own, he doesn't show it.

"Very well," he says briskly. "Get a good night's sleep. No need to be up at dawn with the rest of the workers, but there is much to do in the house to prepare for Her Grace's party."

When you wake the next morning in your bed in the field-worker's dormitory above the carriage house, you find that a servant's livery of dark blue jerkin and black culottes with silver trim is folded over the foot of your bed.

"Smart, eh?" Saeed says from the center of the room, where he has dressed in one of the outfits. Etheldreda stands next to him with a sour expression on her face. You stifle a smile. The livery makes the servants look like little boys and girls. It's good enough for Saeed, who is short for his age anyhow, but Etheldreda is long-limbed and towers over him; her culottes barely go past her knee, and the jerkin sleeves end not just before the wrist but halfway down her forearm.

"Looking good, Baroness," you crack.

"Don't call me that," she hisses, looking around to see if anyone's heard you. When she realizes the three of you are alone, she flashes you a little smile.

You go across the courtyard and into the kitchen, where the cook is barking orders at her staff. With some consternation, you see that Margalit is also working as temporary house staff for the day, looking no more comfortable in her livery than Etheldreda does in hers.

After a morning spent arranging flowers and preparing the sideboards in the dining room, guests begin to arrive. Their carriages pull down the long drive from the main road. While Saeed struggles under the weight of a goose-laden platter that the cook is roaring at him to take into the dining room, you and Etheldreda steal away.

You slip into one of the parlors at the front of the house to watch the nobles disembark from their carriages in front of the main door and enter the grand foyer.

"Do you recognize anyone?" you ask her.

"That's the Marquis de Bois, a minor noble from the western forests. He has no money, but he sings beautifully sad evensongs at the end of the night after the musicians are tired and everyone's exhausted from dancing, so everyone always invites him. That is the Countess of the South Cliff. She sits on the council with the Baroness, she's mad about dance."

You watch the nobles as they are announced and enter the dining hall.

"There goes the Duc de Berry. He's a rare book dealer, he's always commissioning illustrators to create grand volumes for him. My maedaw knew him when she was Baroness."

"What's the difference between a baroness, a countess, and a duke?" you ask.

"Duc," she corrects absently.

"Duke," you attempt to correct yourself.

"Duc," she says again. "Barons and baronesses are minor officials and counselors. In the country we run little villages, in the city they might work at the palace in the government. The counts and countesses control various regions in the countryside. They outrank the baronies and you won't find them in the city, though sometimes they are sent as ambassadors to other kingdoms. The dukes and duchesses rank higher still. They are advisors to the kings and may rule their own cities. It's they and not the kings who command the armies and navies."

"Don't the kings have armies of their own?"

"Maybe in the Narbolin Empire, but not in this part of Elaria. The King is the ruler of the whole kingdom! It wouldn't be right for him to have an army as well!"

"You and you!" Javid bellows from the doorway, stabbing a finger at you. "The nobles are arriving. You're on duty serving the drinks," he commands you. "They're being prepared in the kitchen and will be left on a tray on the service counter. You," he looks at Etheldreda with a particularly nasty expression, "the water closet at the end of the hall has a blockage. Clear it."

Etheldreda grimaces, but as soon as Javid leaves, she rolls her eyes at you. "Maybe I can steal some time and poke around while I'm down at that end of the house," she says, and then heads down the hallway.

You race into the kitchen and see the two trays on the counter between the two service doors to the dining area. Each tray has nine little tumblers of a milky green liquid. You approach to take a tray.

"Not so fast," yells the cook from across the room. How does she see everything that's happening in the kitchen at once? "Those drinks don't have their garnish yet!"

You look quickly around. There's a small ice chest beneath the counter, which has several drawers to the side.

If you open the ice chest, go to section 66.

If you open one of the drawers, go to section 73.

SECTION 72

"Okay," you tell Etheldreda. "We will help you tonight. You know the house and the people who work here. We trust you."

Etheldreda nods, accepting your help and support. You must be careful, you realize. You keep your amulet tucked securely away.

You work the rest of the day, trying to conserve as much energy as possible. At the end of the workday in the fields, as the sun is going down, the field-workers gather in the small courtyard outside the kitchen for a hurried meal of grains and roots. You bed down with the others in dorms above the carriage house.

"The house workers live in small servants' quarters in the basement of the house," Etheldreda tells you as you bunk down. "They stay up later than we do because they have to serve the nobles. We'll have to wait for a few hours."

"All right," you say. "Let's get some rest."

After the noise from the dinner has finally died down, the

three of you creep out of the dorm and across the courtyard. The kitchen lights are low and the house workers seem to have retired. You creep quietly into the darkened kitchen. Near you to your left is a dark staircase leading down, and farther on, a separate staircase leading down that is lit with small candled sconces. At the far end of the kitchen, past the main hearth, on either side of a serving counter are two doors.

"All right, where to?" you ask Etheldreda.

"The household office is at the far end of the main hall," says Etheldreda. "If we go through the door into the dining room, we can slip in quickly."

Just then, from the darkened staircase, there is a boom of wood against wood, and the sound of many voices. You recognize the sound.

"Is there a docking cave below the house?" you ask.

Etheldreda nods. "You can sail straight to Albahr from here in less than an hour."

"Well, someone just came in," you say. You pause and listen to the voices. "About four men, I'd guess."

"They're going to come upstairs," Saeed hisses.

"I think the door off the kitchen will be safe," Etheldreda insists. "But if you want to check out the visitors, I can take you to the docking cave. It's up to you, Krishi."

If you sneak down to the docking cave to investigate, go to section 4.

If you slip through the door at the far end of the kitchen, go to section 14.

SECTION 73

*J*ust below the countertop is a row of square drawers. You open one and see it is filled with black peppercorns and a little silver grinder. The next holds large crystals of pink salt and a small spoon. The third holds large dried star anise.

"Star anise," you say. "That's the thing." With little tongs that lie in the drawer, you pick the star anise up and drop one in each glass. They will add a little zing to the drink and, as long as it's drunk in a reasonable time, won't make the drink bitter.

You carry the tray out into the dining hall, which has been converted into a reception room. The long southern side of the room, to your right, is dominated by an enormous window providing a vista of the rolling sea. Along the window is a wide, cushioned bench where many of the lords and ladies sit, conversing. Others move about the room, including the short and plump Duc de Berry, who moves about the room with a kindly smile, conversing first with one lord and then another and stopping every once in a while to sample a delicacy from one of the trays borne by other servers throughout the room.

Soon he stops by the Baroness and she begins talking to him intensely. He seems uninterested in her, his eyes wandering the room while she talks, every once in a while smiling absently and nodding at her.

You head his way. "Your Grace," you say, inclining your head to the Baroness, "and Your Grace," you say to the Duc, bowing deeper. He notices.

"Well," he says expansively, "what have you brought us?"

The Baroness's eyes light up. "Ah, this is the drink I had when I last attended the Albahri Court under the old King." She takes a glass for herself and hands another to the Duc. She sips from her glass and her eyes close in pleasure. "Perfect!" she says.

The Duc samples his drink and nods as well.

"Sir," you plunge in, "I heard it told that you collect books."

His eyes brighten in interest. "Why yes, my young friend, you have heard properly. And when I cannot find a beautiful enough edition of a book that I love, I commission artisans to make me a new one!"

The Baroness laughs a little brittle laugh. "Yes, the Duc de Berry has given countless hours of work to artists, calligraphers, papermakers, bookbinders—"

"What is your interest in books, my young friend?"

"My maw and daw are scholars," you recount, inventing a story as you speak. "They live in Sky Home, and though I have a love for literature and poetry, I am not much good at studying, so they sent me to Albahr to learn a trade."

The Duc smiles. "And you're learning the Two Rivers dialect! Don't use it when you go back to Sky Home, they won't let you in!" All three of you laugh, the Baroness laughing a little louder than necessary.

"Jean," the Baroness says to the Duc, "let's take a stroll in the garden before it gets crowded."

"What does the weather call for?" the Duc asks Javid as he passes.

"Barish," Javid replies in the Albahrian dialect, with a smile.

"Fetch the Duc appropriate gear for the weather," the Baroness instructs you. "There are cubbies in the foyer. Bottom rack."

You put the tray down and go out the double doors to the foyer. There by the main doors are cubbies containing various items, including hats, gloves, and, in the bottom rack, an umbrella made of sturdy linen treated with some kind of shiny substance and a dark cloth parasol.

Barish, you think. You don't know what this word means, but if you admit that, you'll give your identity away.

If you take the parasol for sun, go to section 74.

If you take the umbrella for rain, go to section 75.

SECTION 74

All you see outside are blue skies, so you grab the parasol and head back inside. You approach the Baroness and the Duc and present the parasol. The Duc smiles a little as he takes it, confused. And the Baroness looks displeased.

"I suppose it is too much to expect our friend from Sky Home to pick up the dialect too quickly," the Duc says kindly. "Barish, my friend, in Albahri means 'rain.'"

"Rain?" you say in surprise. "But it's so clear out!"

"How long did you say you have been in Two Rivers?" the Baroness asks strangely.

"Now, now," says the Duc. "Probably our friend only recently arrived. How is one to know how quickly the spring squalls appear here on the coast?" And, as if on cue, the sky outside opens up in a sudden shower.

The Baroness's eyes narrow. "What did you say your name was?"

"Uh, Pedro, Your Grace," you stammer. "I better get back to

the kitchen. Your Grace. Your Grace." You bow to each of them and beat a hasty retreat toward the kitchen.

"There is something strange about that young person," you hear the Baroness saying as you dissolve back into the crowd.

On your way back to the kitchen, you bump into Saeed. "What's going on? Where's Etheldreda?"

"She made it upstairs," Saeed says, "but I haven't been able to spot her since. I think she's still up there."

"I have to leave, Saeed," you confess. "I think I just blew my cover." You hazard a glance back toward the Baroness, and sure enough she is scanning the room as if she is looking for some-one—you—and talking hurriedly with one of the guards.

"Krishi," Saeed begs. "I can't handle this on my own!"

"You're going to have to," you say, clasping his hands. "They can't even see you talking to me."

Without another word you turn and head into the kitchen. Your exit is masked by all the activity happening there, and you duck behind the rows of carriages lining the drive. You're worried about Saeed, but you know he's been trained well and you have to trust that he will be able to handle the situation. Saeed and Etheldreda are depending on you. The best you can do is get back to the Farmhouse as quickly as possible so they can send reinforcements.

You run down the drive toward the main road. You don't stop running until you reach the cover of the forest.

THE END

SECTION 75

You draw the umbrella out of the rack and head back into the reception room.

The Baroness has moved off toward the window, where a quartet of musicians are setting up their music stands and preparing their instruments. The Duc is standing near a door by the far wall, talking with one of the servers. As you get closer, you see that he is talking to Etheldreda.

"Ah, my young friend!" the Duc says as you approach, taking the umbrella from you. "Thank you for bringing me appropriate protection against our sudden spring rains. The coast has always been rainy in the spring, but I suppose that is why our summer harvests are so bountiful, isn't that right, Dreda?"

Dreda smiles and says, "Yes, Your Grace, though the Lady Lowelia has given much of the arable fields over to horse paddocks now."

"Aha!" the Duc scolds, though still with a smile. "You will not inveigle me into talking politics today! The spring air is beautiful and the Baroness has promised me a walk in the garden." He drifts off toward the Baroness. As the Duc walks away, Saeed passes him with a tray and then quickly swerves, depositing the tray on the nearest side table. He hurries over to you and Etheldreda.

The three of you huddle in the middle of the room, the other partygoers circulating around you.

Etheldreda says, in a low tone impossible to overhear, "I have known the Duc de Berry since I was a little girl and my maedaw was Baroness. He knows the new Baroness is not stewarding the land properly, but none of the governing council is ever keen to depose a noble. We'll have to have solid proof to take our petition to the council."

"Who's on the council now?" you ask.

"It's the Duc, the Countess of the South Cliff, the Baroness herself, Arjun, and the Marquis de Bois."

"The one who sings?"

"Yes, him. He's not a powerful noble, but that's one of the reasons the others put him on the council. Sometimes none of the most powerful dukes has the support and they all want to prevent one another from having too much influence, so they put someone further from the center of power on the council. He still gets a vote though, just like everyone else."

"What about the Countess, what's her agenda?" Saeed asks.

"She's a tough nut. Ever since the Duke of Kulsum's wife, the Duchess Dalilah, made off with his navy, the Countess has been angling to become the new Duchess. But she's unlikely to do anything that will jeopardize her power base here. As Countess of the South Cliff she controls all the shipping routes into Albahr."

"And the smuggling routes too," you add.

"If we can expose the Duke publicly enough, she'll try to save her own skin," says Etheldreda, looking over her shoulder to make sure the coast is clear. "The bad news is that she's moved the office. It isn't where it was when I lived here. It must be upstairs somewhere."

You whistle.

"We don't have a lot to work with and we don't have a lot of time. But besides the King, every other council member is here. If we can get those other three to go against the Baroness, we might not have to even wait until a council meeting."

"Keep serving and keep talking to them," Etheldreda says. "And keep your eye on Javid," she warns. You and Saeed nod and return to work, circulating among the noble guests.

Go to section 76.

SECTION 76

Saeed is called to rejoin the servers, giving you and Etheldreda a chance to case the room. The Countess and the
Marquis are both at the far end of the room, near the musicians,
talking to each other.

"I will try to talk to the Duc as soon as he gets back from
his garden walk," Etheldreda promises. "But in the meantime,
maybe you should try to listen in on that conversation?"

You begin to make your way across the room, but the musicians suddenly strike a dramatic, unified note.

"Gathered nobles and friends!" Javid calls out. "May I present
the world-renowned entertainer, the DAZZLING Zubaydah!"

Your mouth drops open as the nobles part ways to allow the
beautiful Zubaydah to sway into the center of the room. She
stands tall and erect, her broad shoulders covered with a filmy
veil of lavender, her shoulders and chest covered in an exotic
pectoral made of hundreds of miniature shells.

Etheldreda edges her way around the crowd and you are
about to follow suit when Zubaydah suddenly catches your eye.

"Aha," she exclaims. "A young dancer in our midst! Come here!" And she gestures at you imperiously with the crook of one finger. With all eyes on you, you have no choice but to obey.

When you get close to her, she puts one hand on each shoulder and leans in close. "I'm here for the same reason you are, young Whisperer. You're going to buy me some time to sneak upstairs and search for evidence against the Baroness."

Zubaydah turns to the crowd and announces in a loud voice for all to hear, "My friend has agreed to perform the famed Snake Dance!" The crowd erupts with pleasure.

The Marquis de Bois claps his hands. "I've SO wanted to see the Snake Dance performed! I've HEARD so much about it!"

Zubaydah gives you a tight little smile and flutters her fingers at you, then claps to the musicians to signal a start to the music. Etheldreda mouths a silent *What?* You tilt your head slightly toward Zubaydah, willing Etheldreda to follow her as she melts back past the circle of nobles watching you and into the foyer.

The musicians draw a dramatic chord and then glide into an oddly staccato melody, the drumbeat dramatic and irregular. Etheldreda stalks silently after Zubaydah, and you turn to your expectant crowd.

Stay very still and raise your arms above your head, in section 77.

Get down on your hands and knees and prepare to slither, in section 78.

222

SECTION 77

You ou stay completely still. Slowly, as the odd music swells, you raise your arms over your head, and then, with twists and waves in your shoulders, waist, hips, and knees, you begin to make the undulating movements of a snake.

The Marquis is rapt, his eyes on you, as even your wrists and elbows participate in the movement. By instinct, you keep your facial expression completely neutral. That is what a snake would do, you reason.

It is strange to dance with your feet in exactly the same position, but somehow that constraint makes the rest of your movements even more intense and expressive, and when the music comes to an end, you hold your final position for several seconds until the room erupts into applause.

The musicians turn back to playing occasional music and the Marquis strides over to you.

"Now where has Zubaydah gone to?" the Marquis asks.

"I'm not sure," you say. "But I can keep you company until she returns."

"With what might I be able to repay you for your beautiful dance?" the Marquis asks you.

If you say, "Please sing for me later," go to section 55.

If you say, "I want to talk to you about Etheldreda," go to section 56.

SECTION 78

As the music swells you drop to your hands and knees and then slide onto your belly on the polished wooden floor. There are gasps from the nobles. You wriggle forward in what you hope is a snakelike fashion.

"Enough!" cries a woman's voice. The music stops.

You push yourself up and turn. The Countess and the Marquis stand there, their mouths open in horror.

"What is this nonsense?" the Countess demands. "This is not the Snake Dance!"

"It's . . . uh," you stammer, "it's a new dance."

Her eyes narrow with menace.

"It's a new dance," you say, gambling uncertainly, nodding at the musicians to continue. They look as confused as the Marquis.

"Unlikely," she says flatly, "though I like your moxie."

"Javid!" There is a commotion at the entrance from the foyer. Two guards enter, holding Zubaydah tightly between them.

"What is the meaning of this?" Javid asks, appearing, his face as dark as a thundercloud.

"We found her upstairs sneaking through the rooms," the guard says.

"Aha!" Javid exclaims, jabbing a finger at Zubaydah and then at you. "A plot! We'll see what the Baroness has to say!"

Another guard enters, this time with the struggling Etheldreda. Javid's mouth opens in dismay.

"Treason," he hisses.

Your heart sinks.

THE END

SECTION 79

You and Etheldreda make your way up the stairs into the long upstairs corridor. Light floods into the gallery downstairs to your right, and music and the noise of conversation drift up from the party below. To your left, the corridor is quiet and enclosed, with three doors on the north side and great windows on the south side.

"There's no way of telling when the Baroness and the Duc will come back from their garden stroll," she says in a low tone. "We have to be quick."

"All right, where do we start the search?" you ask.

Etheldreda pauses, lost in thought. "The first door was where the housekeeper's office used to be; maybe the Baroness is using it as a private office now? The second door is the most sumptuous guest room, normally where the most high-ranking visiting nobility stay. The last door is the baronial suite."

If you want to investigate the luxurious guest room, go to section 50.

If you want to check out the baronial suite, go to section 51.

If you want to look into the old housekeeper's office, go to section 80.

SECTION 80

You creep into the room that was once the housekeeper's office and close the door quietly behind you. So far, so good.

The room is medium-sized, with a window facing west that opens out onto the main entrance of the house. It is occupied by a desk and several shelves full of ledgers and books.

"This must be where she keeps her correspondence and records," Etheldreda says.

"Why don't you check out the desk," you suggest, "and I'll see if there's anything in the books and ledgers."

You search for a few minutes, and then Etheldreda whistles. "I think I found something, Krishi," she says. She holds a ledger out to you.

"What am I looking at?" you ask her, scanning the columns of spidery entries.

"These are the names of ships," she says, pointing. "And these are descriptions of arms: 'forty bronze-tipped spears, seven iron swords,' and so on. She's the one smuggling weapons in. Even if it doesn't say where, we have proof she is aware of the smuggling. She'll crack under pressure!"

"I'm not sure," you say. "Maybe we should keep searching."

"It's risky," she says. "Who knows when Javid will notice we're gone!"

If you want to look in the guest room, go to section 50.

If you want to look in the baronial suite, go to section 51.

If you want to take the ledger book and confront the Baroness, go to section 58.

SECTION 81

Your eyes keep returning to the third, starry barque.

You approach it with your hands outstretched. The space around it gets bluer and bluer.

"Krishi, I don't know about this," says Arjun. "Krishi!" His voice sounds like it's coming from far away, or like you are hearing it through water.

Your hands touch the side of the barque. You gaze down into its jeweled depths. You feel an air current beneath you, and you are lifted up.

You feel your body pass through the stone and rise above the Heart of the Storm. You stretch your arms out and rise higher, looking down over the island. Down in the Citadel you can see Suraj scrambling to gather frightened students around him. Up on the ramparts, you see Sandhya gathering the older students to fight.

As you rise higher, you see the ships approaching the Citadel, their cannons and spikes at the ready. Rising farther still you can see Dev and Chandh Sahib and the others, landing at a rocky cove, west of the city.

Somehow you realize you could slide down any of these threads, be anywhere.

But how? You remain suspended in space, threads weaving down into multiple realities, but you do not know how to return to the world you left. You remain above, watching the story happen, but no longer in it.

THE END

SECTION 82

"They're too close," you decide. "We can get to the kitchens quicker and make sure everyone is safe."

Arjun nods curtly in agreement.

"All right," says Suraj. "Everyone stay close. We won't use the main corridor. There's a service entrance to the kitchen just up the little stairs by the stage."

You make your way quickly as a group to the opposite side of the Great Hall. You notice that Arjun has taken Dimple's hand and that the little girl is huddling close to him. While you are watching, he turns his head, catches your eye, gives you an impudent wink.

Your cheeks burn a little but you smile back and hurry on.

Suraj reaches the door and gestures the students forward. "Krishi, you and Arjun go first and get the students into the root cellar. I'll come in last, to make sure that no soldiers see us."

As you and Arjun—still holding Dimple's hand—slip into the empty kitchen, you hear a crash as soldiers burst into the Great Hall.

233

"Go," hisses Suraj. "Go! Go! Go!" The students, ten of them, hurry into the kitchen while Suraj runs back out into the Great Hall, takes a flying leap off the stage, and charges toward the soldiers, shouting.

He's creating a distraction for you! You quickly roll back the jute rug that covers the trapdoor to the root cellar. "Come on," you call to the children, lifting the trapdoor up. Arjun guides Dimple down first, and then the younger children all file down obediently. "Someone is going to have to stay up here to roll the carpet back," you say to Arjun.

"And that someone is me," says Arjun. You open your mouth to protest, but Arjun puts one finger on your lips. "No, Krishi. You have to hide with the students until the coast is clear. Then you can slip out of the Citadel and make for the forest. They're going to need someone who knows the Citadel and who can protect them in the forest. That someone is you, not me. The pirates are going to want a prisoner who is as valuable as possible. And that's me, not you."

He leans forward and kisses you gently on each cheek. "I can't let you do this," you stammer.

"You have no choice," he says. "I am ordering you to follow my command. I am Arjun, the King of Albahr." He smiles sadly. "Dev sent me here to hide me, didn't you guess?"

Now you realize what Arjun meant. He will be safer with the pirates because he is more valuable to them alive. You nod silently and climb down the ladder into the root cellar. Arjun closes the door behind you, and you hear the sound of the jute rug being rolled back over the door. The streams of light disappear and you are left with the students in the darkness.

"Around me," you whisper, and you feel the students crouching together.

"Now what?" asks Dimple.

"Now we wait," you say. "Until nightfall. When the soldiers sleep, I will sneak back out and find a way for us to the forest."

You can only hope that Arjun knows what he is doing, and that he stays safe. In the darkness, the hours slowly unravel.

THE END

SECTION 83

$\int$uraj is going to have to defend himself. You swallow hard. As you back away toward the staircase, Suraj suddenly drops flat to the ground in the same move you saw Saeed use earlier during your combat class. The soldiers pause for one split second and Suraj spins on his shoulders, lashing out with both legs at once, knocking two of the soldiers back into the walls.

Whether he is dancing on a stage or taking on a hostile force, you can never take your eyes off Suraj—he's an artist—but you can't stay and watch. You turn and follow Arjun and the young students down to the docks.

Some of the kids are crying. You wish you knew the charm Suraj used when he threw his voice straight into your ear. Come to think of it, you're fairly sure Sandhya has used magic to quiet down a room of rowdy pupils at some point in the past as well.

"Okay, quiet, everyone," Arjun says in a dramatic whisper as you enter the docking cavern. You smile in spite of yourself. Arjun is still holding on to little Dimple's hand. The girl is clearly frightened, but she is huddling close to Arjun.

The cavern is deserted, but you see the small Narbolin sloops beside the massive chain used to close the harbor off.

"Come!" you call out, shepherding everyone over to the eastern wall where the massive tapestry hangs, depicting fire being thrown at invaders.

"The teaching tapestry!" Dimple says.

You smile at her, nodding, and then reach out and touch the tapestry. You've looked at it so many times in lessons, and yet—yes, there it is: hovering in the sky, amid the fireballs being flung down from the ramparts by the Whisperers, nearly invisible against the deep purple hue of the darkening sky, is a black shape you recognize.

"The lunar barque!" exclaims Arjun.

"Bark?" asks Dimple, confused.

Arjun laughs. "Barque. It's a boat that's used to bear the king up into the sky."

"Will the boat rescue us? Are we going to go in it up in the sky?" Dimple asks, perking up in excitement for the first time since you were all in the Great Hall.

You reach out and cover the dark boat with your left palm, then reach back with your right. You pull energy through like you did before. The tapestry quivers a little under your hand. Just as you hoped: *the barques work both ways.* With magic, that is.

"Time to go," you say.

Dimple takes your right hand and walks toward the tapestry. She reaches out to touch it and her hand goes through. She looks back at you in wonder. You nod. She hesitates. She looks back at Arjun. He nods. She walks through the tapestry. One of the other students inhales in shock, looking at you with wide eyes.

"You're next, Hasan," you say to him, and reach out your hand. He takes it and walks through. One by one, each of the students takes your hand, and with your left hand on the image of the barque you shepherd them through, sending them to safety. Soon it's only you and Arjun.

He stops in front of you, looking into your eyes. "You're not coming," he realizes.

"An object cannot manifest magic on its own," you say, repeating the lesson you learned. "A human must channel it."

"Krishi, there's something I have to tell you."

You smile. "There's no time, Arjun. You have to go."

He reaches out and touches your cheek. "Take care of yourself, Krishi. I've got the kids. I'll keep them safe."

You smile. You know he will. As for what he wanted to tell you, at least you have something to look forward to.

Still holding your hand, Arjun walks into the tapestry, and you feel his hand dissolve into the darkness. You are left alone in the cavern. Should you head back to where you last saw Suraj? Or hide here and wait?

If you look around the docking cavern for a place to hide, go to section 27.

If you run back up the stairs to the main level, go to section 84.

SECTION 84

You hesitate. You can't leave Suraj behind.

You run toward the struggle. One of the soldiers spins around and swings the hilt of his sword at you. You try to duck, but it hits you in the side of the head. You go down, smarting, seeing stars.

"Krishi!" Suraj cries and jumps toward you. Two soldiers quickly restrain him, pinning his arms behind his back. One soldier kicks the back of his knees, forcing him down to the ground.

You push yourself up to your hands and knees, your eyes watering. Sandhya was wrong—it was good practice learning how to take a hit. You breathe heavily and wait. The soldier approaches you and, at what you hope is exactly the right moment, you kick out. You catch the soldier's shin and he yelps, jumping back, but it isn't enough. The other two have a blade against Suraj's neck.

"Enough!" cries out a voice, and a small, slender man with silver hair and gray eyes strides into view. "Who is this little warrior?" he asks in a deceptively smooth voice. "Ready to lay down your life for your dear teacher?"

"Leave Krishi alone, Zephyr!" shouts Suraj, straining without success against the soldiers who hold him.

"Oh, there'll be time enough to deal with *you*," says Zephyr before turning to Suraj. When he nods at the soldiers, they force Suraj to his feet. "But first you and I are going to have a long conversation, my old friend."

The soldiers force Suraj into the great hall, and Zephyr follows. The other soldiers restrain you. What now? You remember the lesson: wait for your moment. You're in trouble, and so is Suraj. You have no idea where Sandhya is and you can only hope that Arjun and the children got away safely.

You'll keep your eyes open for an opportunity. But for now, it's

THE END

SECTION 85

ou eye the choppy waves from the shallows. As much as you want to be able to help Sandhya, and Suraj and the other students, you might be able to have the most impact by damaging the Narbolin ships.

"How much do you trust me?" asks the Duchess, sidling up beside you.

"It's your boat, Duchess. You know it best."

She lets out a little whoop and scrambles up the little rope ladder, stepping into the nearest small craft. She leans back and gives you a hand up.

"I knew you were smart. We'll have to row out. Once we're in the harbor, maybe you could . . ." she points down toward the water and makes a little mystical twirl with her fingers.

You laugh. "I don't know. I can try."

It takes all the strength the two of you have to pull the oars through the water. As you bend to your oar you try with your mind to tap into the energy of the water and the energy of the oar. You try to build speed, but can't manage it. Your training so far at the Citadel has been more mundane. You are barely scratching the surface of the mystical arts.

"All right, heave ho, little one!" calls out the Duchess, and your little craft emerges from the shallows and into the harbor.

Ahead through the mist you see the breakwater. The Duchess unfurls the sail.

"If we tack hard starboard," shouts the Duchess over the roar of the water crashing against the base of the cliff, "I think we can pull alongside the Narbolin ships. We might have a shot at reaching them undetected. It's hard to tell whether they'd be looking out or not. We're in one of their ships, too."

You look out to the galleons. You aren't sure this is a good idea. The Duchess follows your gaze.

"Though we might still be able to catch up with Chandh Sahib and your friends. If I tack port when we pass the breakwater, there's a fast-channel that will carry us right past them into open sea. Even if they saw us, I doubt they would be able to catch up."

Those you left behind in the Citadel are still on your mind, but you have to be strategic in your thinking.

If you want to sneak up to the Narbolin ships, go to section 28.

If you think it's wiser to make a run for it, go to section 29.

SECTION 86

"I'm sorry, Duchess," you say slowly. "I know you would probably feel better out at sea, but we can't just leave Suraj and Sandhya and the other students here. We have to figure out what happened to them."

She smiles and claps you on the back. "I wouldn't have it any other way, Krishi! Can't leave a sailor behind. Can I convince you to take this then?" And she brandishes the stiletto again.

"I better stick with what I know," you say, holding up your hands.

"All right," she says, tucking the long blade back into the sheath in her boot. "How do we do this?"

"There was fighting in the main corridor when I came down here. That would be the most direct route back. Plus Suraj was up that way. On the other hand, Sandhya was taking the older students up to the ramparts to fight. There's a service staircase on the far side of the cavern that runs up to the ramparts."

"It's your turf, Krishi. What do you think we should do?"

If you think it would better to head back to the main corridor and try to find Suraj, go to section 87.

If you want to head up the service staircase to the ramparts, go to section 88.

SECTION 87

Stealthily you creep up the open stairs from the docks, listening carefully as you go. You are amazed that the Duchess, in her big boots and velvet jacket, is somehow managing to be as quiet as you are, with your linen clothing and years of Whisperer training.

You near the top of the stairs and are about to enter the main corridor when the Duchess seizes you by the back of your tunic and pulls you back into the darkness.

Though you are surprised, you stay quiet. You watch a Narbolin soldier creep down the corridor past the opening, himself trying to be stealthy. Unlike the other soldiers you saw earlier, he is clad in black leather garments. Also unlike the other Narbolins, he has long silver—nearly white—hair, though he seems as young as the others. You look back at the Duchess, her eyes narrowing. She holds one finger to her lips.

You wait a few minutes until the man has crept past you, and then you enter the main corridor. It's completely deserted. The four soldiers you saw circling Suraj are slumped against the walls beside the double doors leading to the Great Hall. You breathe a sigh of relief.

"That's bad news," the Duchess says. "Zephyr. One of the meanest pirates on the seas. If he's with the Narbolins, we better step carefully."

"Maybe Suraj got away," you say, hoping you are right.

"Where would he go?" the Duchess asks.

You think for a minute.

If you think Suraj hid in the kitchens, go to section 89.

If you think Suraj must have been captured, go to section 90.

SECTION 88

"It's too dangerous to go back to the main corridor. Not many people know about the service staircase," you inform the Duchess.

The Duchess nods curtly and the two of you head across the cavern for the small staircase. As you enter, you can't help but feel a little uneasy. The staircase is narrow and turns in a tight spiral as it climbs up. You listen as hard as you can as you climb, but if there is combat happening inside the rest of the castle, you can't hear it. Could the fight be over already?

You gesture silently, and the two of you climb the staircase. The staircase twists in the dark and you move as quietly as you can, though the Duchess's scabbard brushes against the stone every once in a while, sending echoes up and down the spiral. It's impossible to say how far the sound travels, but you imagine you are pretty insulated because you can't hear anything from inside the castle. Then, when you imagine you are close to the top, you hear the door being dragged open. A thin stream of light enters the spiral.

"Should we go down?" a voice asks.

"I don't think so," purrs another voice, soft and full of malice. "It's a spiral staircase. The perfect place for an ambush. We already sealed the door at the docks. Lock this side and bar it. If they're in there, they have nowhere to go. Perhaps we can let them out in a day or two. By then the fight will have gone out of them."

You quickly make a break for the top, but the tightly turning spiral doesn't allow you much time to pick up speed. You hear the door clang shut and the heavy bar drawn across it.

You hear the Duchess breathing heavily. You are in pitch dark.

Maybe they will let you out in a day or two and you can figure out what to do next. You don't allow yourself to dwell on the alternative.

THE END

SECTION 89

You snap your fingers.

"The kitchens," you say. "There's a root cellar that you can hide in as long as you have a lookout to roll the carpet back over the trapdoor."

"You think he has an accomplice?" the Duchess asks.

"I'm not sure, but if he did get away, that's the one place I could think that he would be."

The two of you stealthily climb the narrow stone staircase that leads back to the main corridor. You crouch low and peek around the corner. There's no one there. Sprinting as quietly as you can, you slide the doors of the Great Hall a fraction and slip inside, the Duchess right behind you.

"There's an entrance to the kitchen at the far end," you whisper. The hall is deserted and you feel a little sad, thinking of all the meals and classes you and your friends partook of in here. The Citadel feels ghostly without the sounds of hollering kids at mealtime.

The two of you creep across the room and slip into the

kitchen. As soon as you enter, two Narbolin soldiers come in from the opposite side.

"More, sir!" one of them hollers down the hall. The other one makes a jump for you. The Duchess leaps in front of you, crouching low, her rapier already drawn.

"All right, matey," she drawls in her best pirate-captain voice. "Let's have at it!"

Another man enters. It's the silver-haired man you saw earlier, the one the Duchess called Zephyr. He's slim and small, only a little taller than you. "Well," he says in a smooth low voice. "Another little chickadee." The black leather armor he wears looks like it will blunt any blow from your unarmed techniques. Now you wish you had accepted the Duchess's stiletto.

You remember her admonishment: Whisperers use any weapon that's at hand. Well, here goes nothing. You swipe a meat tenderizer off the counter and swing it at him. He falls back, surprised. You advance and spin, hurling the tenderizer at him and grabbing a cast-iron pan off the hearth. As he stumbles back to avoid the tenderizer, you spin again and complete your windmill punch. The pan catches him solidly on the side of his head with a clang to the helmet. His eyes widen in shock.

"Nice work," he slurs with grudging admiration, and then his eyes roll back and he collapses in a heap.

"And that's how you do it," says the Duchess, clapping her hands. You see she has already dispatched her opponent. Your face clouds with worry when you see the man lying prone. "He's not dead," the Duchess says. "But we probably better get him stitched up. He'll have a scar, no doubt, but that's a story to tell his grandkids."

"Suraj?" you call down into the darkness after you lift the trapdoor. "Are you there?"

"Krishi!" he calls out with relief as he climbs up. "You look like you've been able to take care of things pretty well without me!"

"We need to get that one tied up quickly," says the Duchess. "Zephyr is dangerous. If he's here, then he's the one responsible for that fleet. A right valuable prisoner, Krishi. Well done."

Suraj finds a coil of jute, and with a series of intricate knots, binds up the inert Zephyr.

"We have to find Sandhya!" you say.

The Duchess bends down and lifts Zephyr's head up by the chin to look at him. "He's out cold," she says. "You really clocked him." She draws her rapier again. "Let's go."

Suraj is examining the other soldier. "I'll stay and stitch him up, and hold him prisoner as well. Bring me the medical kit," he says, gesturing toward the white wooden box that hangs by a small chain near the doorway.

You bring him the kit and leave him. You advance slowly into the hallway, the Duchess just behind you. From the far end, where a staircase leads to the upper floors, you hear a commotion. Both of you crouch into fighting stances, but you breathe a sigh of relief. The people coming down the stairs wear Whisperer robes. At the end of the group is Sandhya, her hair loose from its binding. She is bleeding just slightly from a small cut above her left eye.

"Krishi! Thank the shining moon!"

She half-runs toward you and engulfs you in an embrace. You stiffen in surprise. You can't ever remember Sandhya being so affectionate. She pulls back then, still holding you tightly by the shoulders.

"Are you all right? Where is Arjun? What about the children?"

"They're safe," you say. "We got them out."

She sees the Duchess then and her eyes widen in surprise. "You! What about Chandh Sahib and the others?"

"I got them through," the Duchess says. "And then came back to keep an eye on you."

"And a good thing that was," you add, smiling at her in gratitude. "Sandhya, what now?"

"We have the Citadel under control," she says, "and the invaders locked up. I want to talk to the leader."

"Suraj has him," you say, "in the kitchen. We tied him up with another soldier."

"Krishi took him out," says the Duchess.

Sandhya smacks your back in affection. "I knew you were paying attention in my fighting classes! All right, let's have a conversation with our captain and find out precisely why an invading force was sent to the inviolate Citadel. It's too bad that the King of Albahr is still missing, but in either case, I believe the Narbolin Emperor will have some explaining to do."

THE END

SECTION 90

"It's too quiet," you say. "Either Suraj is safely hidden or else they have him. Either way, I think it's smarter for us to get out of here while we still can."

"Live to fight another day," the Duchess says, nodding her head. "Bide your time and strike back. A sound strategy. You would have made a good pirate."

"What makes you think I might not still become one?" you say with a smile. You take one last look around you. This place has been your home for years and you don't know when you'll come back.

"Don't look to the past, Krishi," says the Duchess, interrupting your reverie. "It's time to look to the future, whatever it may hold."

You drag the back of your hand across your eyes. "Come," you say and start down the hallway away from the Great Hall and toward the kitchens. You pass by the kitchens with a pang, hoping again that Suraj has managed to hide himself. Just past the entrance to the kitchen is a staircase leading down five or six steps into the kitchen courtyard. At the end, through the vegetable garden, lies the path that runs to the forested interior.

It's real to you now. You are leaving the Citadel to the Narbolins. But the Duchess is right. You have to make it back to Arjun and the other students. Then you can plan. If Sandhya and Suraj are still alive, they may find a way to you as well.

All is not lost. An ending is never really the end.

THE END

SECTION 91

You look back toward the cliffs, now barely visible in the rain coming down.

You have pulled alongside the galleon. "It's time to decide, Krishi," the Duchess says, urgently.

"We go up," you say. "If there's a way to solve this with minimal violence or destruction, then that's what we should do."

"Spoken like a true Whisperer," she says admiringly.

"Also it's more efficient, and would yield greater rewards."

"Also spoken like a true Whisperer."

"Who are you, Duchess?" you ask. "And how is it you know so much about the Whisperers? And what is a duchess doing in the storm, getting ready to try to commandeer a Narbolin ship?"

"Ah matey," she says, clapping you on the back. "These are stories for other days, warmer ones, by a fire, a goblet of fiery drink in one hand and a full pipe in the other."

The Duchess reaches down into a locker at the bow of the boat and pulls out a grappling hook with a length of line. She swings the hook around in a practiced arc and then hurls it up to the rail. You strain to hear any sound of it landing through the rain on the water and the roar of the surf, but it's lost to you. You pray the sailors on board the ship didn't hear it either.

"Move out," commands the Duchess, and you immediately take hold of the thick line and twist the bottom around your ankle.

With great effort, you begin pulling yourself hand over hand up the line, shimmying your ankles up as you advance. You feel the pull on the line as the Duchess grabs hold from beneath you. As you near the top, you slow for a little, trying to figure out what's happening on the deck. You hear some shouting, but otherwise it's hard to tell. The rope is wet in your hands and your arms are singing with the effort of climbing, so you figure there's no choice but to climb on. You pull yourself up over the rail with one smooth movement and somersault onto the deck, keeping low.

A quick scan of the deck reveals that the crew is doing everything they can to keep the boat off the breakwater, but still keep it close enough to the harbor. Likely whoever is commanding the expedition ordered it so. The officers are up on the aft deck barking orders. You gesture to the Duchess, who has climbed up on the deck behind you.

The two of you creep through the rain up the stairs to the aft deck. The Captain is at the wheel, and the mate, just beside him, is uncoiling one of the lines.

"Who the blazes are you?" the Captain demands, and the Duchess answers him with the quickest jab to the face you've ever seen. For a moment, you're not even sure she landed the punch, but the man sways on his feet in the rain for just a moment and then crumples to the deck.

The mate cries out and makes a move toward her, but you lunge forward, pulling the blade from his scabbard and holding it out toward him. "I think we're done here," you say coldly.

He raises his hands in surrender, and the Duchess lashes his hands behind his back with the line he was uncoiling.

"I thought Whisperers don't use weapons," she says with a smile.

"On the contrary," you say. "A Whisperer uses the tool that is available and needed for the job."

"ALL RIGHT, LADDIES," the Duchess shouts over the storm to the men on the deck. "THERE'S A NEW CAPTAIN ON BOARD! WHO WANTS TO GET OUT OF HERE AND GO HOME?"

The men pause in their work and look at each other with wild eyes and then back up at the Duchess. This couldn't possibly work. Or could it?

"Aye, Captain!" shouts a grizzled sailor on the portside. "We'll sink against those rocks if we don't pull out to sea!"

"Then pull out to sea is what we'll do, laddies!" She begins barking orders you can't even understand, but the crew, down to a man, fall in line. A few are grumbling. You'll keep your eyes on them.

"What now, Duchess?" you ask.

"What indeed, young Krishi. The Citadel is fallen, I fear. But you got the children to safety, and Arjun too. We have a ship and a crew and a lot of open sea. It's enough to bide our time and come up with a plan."

For the moment, at least, you allow yourself to feel hopeful.

THE END

SECTION 92

"It's too risky," you say. "We're no good to our friends in the Citadel if we can't stop this invasion. We sink the boat, and then we try to sink another. If the troops are trapped here at the Citadel with no way ashore and no way to communicate with the other forces, then that's a bigger victory than if we ourselves escape."

The Duchess nods somberly, knowing that you have made the more difficult choice. It is a choice that will bind you to the fate of Sandhya, Suraj, and the other Whisperers, whatever that fate may be.

"So be it," the Duchess says, reaching down into a locker at the bow of the small craft and retrieving several large and wicked-looking metal tools, one with a long curved hook and another maul-like bludgeon. She hands the hook to you. "I smash at the waterline, then you swing that hook in and pull at the boarding. If we can create a gash wide enough, the water will rush in. Repeat as necessary. It's not going to be easy, and will become harder still if someone gets wise to us."

You gesture for her to begin, and she swings the maul in a wide arc and bashes at the hull. It takes her two or three tries, but eventually a tear opens in the sealed wood. You swing the hook and crack in, but as you pull you realize it is going to require much greater strength than you have.

The wood was once a living thing, you think. Perhaps there is still some life in it. Can you coax it mentally to split and open? It is not a magic you have studied much. As another option, the hook is in your hand. Perhaps you could increase its strength and pull? There's no path you feel fully confident about, but the longer the two of you are at it, the greater the chance that one of the sailors will notice you.

If you decide to focus your mind on the wood
in hopes of weakening it, go to section 30.

If you think it's better to strengthen the hook, go to section 31.

SECTION 93

"*C*ome with me," you say to Arjun. "There's no time to waste."
You run toward the Great Hall but you're stopped by a
great thundering boom. The doors burst open and Suraj comes
out, followed by several students.

"Krishi! What is going on?!"

You skid to a halt. "It's not just a blockade, Suraj! Narbolins
are attacking."

Suraj looks at you in disbelief.

"It's true," Arjun says authoritatively. "I saw them too."

Suraj swivels to face Arjun, the disbelief turning to alarm.

"Well, I didn't see them, exactly. But I was there when
Krishi saw them. They're out there. They're on their way."

"All right," Suraj says, all business now. "I have to take the
children down into the cellars to protect them. Arjun, you must
come with me; it's not safe up here."

"I'm staying with Krishi," Arjun declares, stepping closer to
you and putting his hand on your arm. What is he thinking,
disobeying a master?

Surprisingly, Suraj assents. "Fine. But Arjun is your responsibility, Krishi."

You pause, even though time is short. Why does Arjun need this special protection, and why should the rules bend for him? You agreed to protect Arjun, but maybe you did not understand what you were agreeing to.

If you insist that Arjun go with Suraj, go to section 95.

If you feel Arjun would be safer with you, go to section 96.

SECTION 94

"We've got to find Sandhya first," you say. "She's the combat master, she'll know what to do."

You lead Arjun through the kitchens and hang a sharp left to reach the stairwell that leads to the second floor. You exit the stairwell into a narrow dark corridor that leads forward and then divides again.

"All the masters have offices up here. It's literally a maze."

"What do you mean?" asks Arjun, confused.

"The offices are in the maze. The only way to meet with any of the masters is to stay truly focused on the time and purpose of your meeting, and who you're meeting with. It's not just offices, either. If you lose focus, you can wind up literally *anywhere*," you tell Arjun. "The maze is charmed. It's a test."

A cloud passes over Arjun's eyes. "That could be dangerous, Krishi. Maybe we should just go on and light the beacon while we still have time!"

If you run up to light the beacon, go to section 10.

If you think you can risk the maze, go to section 99.

SECTION 95

"Arjun," you say with determination. "You have to go with Suraj. It's safer. You cannot be put in danger."

Arjun's face sets stubbornly. "What did Dev Acharya tell you?" he asks accusingly.

"Krishi," Suraj cuts in, his voice low and insistent. "It isn't the time for this. We have the advantage at the moment, but it evaporates with each passing second."

A rebellious blush flares up on Arjun's face, but you take hold of his shoulders and shove him, more roughly than you wish you had, toward Suraj.

"Go," you command. Suraj grasps his wrist and half-pulls him down the hallway.

"Krishi," he calls back in alarm. "Krishi, be careful!"

You wave a little as they disappear back into the Great Hall.

You pause. The sky outside the two great windows high on the wall at the north and south ends of the Great Hall has gone dark. You hear another boom. They must be lobbing cannonballs at the walls! So this isn't a ground invasion after all. That gives you some sense of relief in that it seems Suraj and the others will be safe, as long as they can find a secure hiding place.

Suddenly you hear Sandhya's voice, amplified throughout the hallway, calling out, "Students! Those who can fight, report to the ramparts! Those who are not prepared, meet Suraj in the Great Hall!"

The ramparts! You turn and sprint to the south window. On the left wall beside it is a display case hiding a secret arch behind it. The arch opens to a steep spiral staircase up to the ramparts. If you can make it there, you can use it to meet Sandhya!

You skid to a stop in front of the display case and pull it back. It's so heavy! You heave it again and feel it creak open slowly. Just then, you hear a cry behind you as more than a dozen Narbolin soldiers burst into the hallway. They quickly overpower you, pulling you back out through the secret passage.

"Well, well, well." You hear a smooth voice approaching. The soldiers spin around, and you see a slender man approaching. His silver hair falls past his shoulders. He's clad all in black and moving, it seems to you, like a cat. He approaches, lifting your chin with one long finger and fixing you in his gray gaze. "We've got a little chickadee."

You sigh, knowing your move to help will now lead the Narbolins directly to the Whisperers.

"And what's this?" the man says in mocking surprise, turning slowly toward the archway. "A little staircase, have we? And where does one suppose it leads?"

He turns his gaze back to you, blinking slowly and exaggeratedly. He scrapes one fingernail along your jawbone as he draws his saber as loudly as possible out of its metal-lined scabbard.

However this ends, you think to yourself with growing dread, *it's not going to be pleasant.*

THE END

SECTION 96

You take Arjun's hand firmly and nod curtly.

"He'll be safe with me, Suraj," you say with confidence.

Suraj and the younger students all disappear back inside the Great Hall.

"All right," you say to Arjun, hoping you sound more confident than you feel. "Our best chance is probably to get up to the beacon on the highest tower and light it. If we light it quickly, there's a chance that Chandh Sahib and the others will see it and send reinforcements."

You both run toward the stairwell at the northern end of the Great Hall. You are running into the darkness when suddenly Sandhya's voice erupts, as if she's right beside you: "Students! Those who can fight, report to the ramparts! Those who are not prepared, meet Suraj in the Great Hall!"

"The ramparts!" you cry out. You turn to Arjun. "Listen! There's a spiral staircase at the southern end of the Hall that leads straight up the ramparts."

"Krishi, no!" Arjun cries out, plucking at the hood on your

cloak as you try to start off toward the other end of the hallway. "Any enemy within the Citadel just now must have ALSO heard her! They're all on their way there right now."

You pause, trying to think a minute, biting your lip in concentration. "Well, either she miscalculated how soon they would breach the dock, or her announcement was a deliberate trap!"

"How well do you know her?"

"She didn't miscalculate," you say confidently. "The announcement was a trap."

"So now the question is, is she using the students as bait? Would the Narbolins be more likely to come to the Great Hall to take prisoners or try to surprise her on the ramparts?"

"You're confusing me," you say. "Does Sandhya want the Narbolins to come down here or is she trying to draw them to her? What does she think they are going to do?"

Arjun waves a dismissive hand. "It doesn't matter. It matters what kind of trap we're going to set."

If you stay at the Great Hall and try to rig up an ambush by the doors, go to section 97.

If you try to use the hidden staircase to get up to the ramparts and get a jump on them, go to section 98.

SECTION 97

"We stay here at the Great Hall," you say.

"Fine then," says Arjun, surveying the area. "What if we move that big table over to the doors? We can use it as a barricade."

You work together to drag the heavy table toward the doorway when suddenly a dozen soldiers burst into the corridor at the southern end. One of them calls out and four of them run toward you.

"Get back!" you shout at Arjun. He jumps behind the table as the four men advance on you. They circle you warily, once or twice jabbing toward you with their swords. This doesn't look good.

"Hey Corporal!" Arjun is shouting from the other side of the table. One soldier's eyes narrow and he lunges toward Arjun. Arjun swipes the huge stoneware jug of flowers from the table and chucks it right at the Corporal's head, tiger-lily-and-bird-of-paradise arrangement included.

You dearly hope the crack you hear when the jug strikes

the Corporal is the jug breaking and not his skull, but in either case he's stopped short. He stands there a moment, swaying, himself like a lily swaying on the stalk, and then, slowly, as if he is moving through honey, he rocks back on his heels and pitches over.

Time starts moving again. You shout a battle cry and grab one soldier's forearm, pulling him toward you and spinning, using the momentum to lift and strike him with a back kick. You complete the movement with a left hook that knocks another soldier on his back.

Still shouting, still spinning, you grasp the fourth soldier by the forearm, step down in the last and fastest part of the spin and release the soldier to smack against the wall. He stays there for a moment, his arms spread-eagle, and then, with a slow, whining squeak, slides down the wall into a crumpled heap.

"Wow," says Arjun. "We just kicked their asses."

"Such vulgar language!" you cry, teasing him.

He smiles. "I'm not that proper, am I?" he asks.

"You're that proper," you say.

His brow wrinkles.

"What's wrong?" you ask.

"It's quiet," he says. "It means the fight is over."

You whistle. How is Arjun so weak, yet so crafty about military matters? "Maybe Sandhya won."

"I don't think so," Arjun says, coming around the table slowly. "If they won, then wouldn't things be getting back to normal? They'd be coming down with the prisoners, right?"

"The Narbolins have the Citadel!" you exclaim.

Arjun grows fearful. "Krishi, we have to get out of here right now," he says, something like desperation filling his voice.

"You're going nowhere!" cuts in a chillingly pleasant voice. A smiling man emerges from the darkness at the far end of the hallway, flanked by soldiers at the ready. "And who are these little birds, caught in my net?"

Something about the way he enunciates each word fully sends a chill up your spine.

"This little bit is a wee whispering Whisperer. But this," he purrs, turning to Arjun, who has grown stiff and ashen at his approach, "this is Arjun, so-called King of Albahr. Your *Majesty*," he says, pouring as much of an insulting tone as he can manage into the word, "the Emperor of Narbolis has been longing for an interview with you."

With a sharp tilt of his head, two of the soldiers charge forward and take custody of Arjun, dragging him off, his head raised stubbornly, but his lip trembling in fear.

"Now, you," says the silver-haired man, with menace. "What are we to do with you?"

Your eyes fill with tears, but not because you are afraid. You have lost Arjun, whose identity and need for protection are now known to you, cementing what you've lost. You have disappointed Dev Acharya. For reasons you understand, and reasons you know you cannot yet fathom, that seems like a fate worse than death.

THE END

SECTION 98

You ou snap your fingers.

"No way the Narbolins are going to come here and then try to sneak around. They're going to go where the fight is."

"What if it's pirates?"

"I'd give ninjas to pirates that Sandhya and the senior students can handle a pirate crew. Trained soldiers, that's something else."

"But the Whisperers are trained in all kinds of combat styles, isn't that true?"

"Sure," you say slowly, "but mostly the technique of the Whisperers is to operate in the shadows. We're great at subterfuge and sneaking, but if there are forty armed Narbolins coming right at us? Well," you pause, "we're not really trained for that."

"All right then," he says. "Subterfuge. If the Narbolins are heading up to the ramparts—"

"Then we need to get there before them!" you cry in a rush.

"No, Krishi," says Arjun, looking at you quizzically. "Subter-fuge, remember? We need to get there after them."

Understanding dawns on you. You scan the hallway. It's lined with display cases of swords and spears that are usable weapons. On the other hand, you're best with your hands. But Arjun can't fight. "The banner," you announce.

Arjun's eyes narrow as he considers the length of the dark blue banner that hangs down the length of the hall. It bears delicate glass globes containing glowing blue stones. They provide a subtle evening light for the walkway when daylight fades.

"The banner," he says in agreement.

You climb up onto a heavy table pushed against the wall and detach the banner. Working quickly, you slide each glass globe down. Then you run across the hallway, climb up on a chair, and detach the other end of the banner. Looping the banner loosely around your forearm, you and Arjun make your way down to the southern end of the hallway.

"The staircase is behind this display case," you say to Arjun when you reach a vitrine. It contains a sculpture of a longboat on rough seas, pitching beneath two golden metallic suns.

"The solar barque," Arjun says brightly as you pull at the corner. You pause and look at him for an extra moment, piecing something together in your mind.

The display case is very heavy and it takes all of your and Arjun's strength to pull it away from the wall. When you finally get it free, a darkened recess is revealed, and a staircase within. You creep up the spiral stairs, listening hard for signs of danger.

"It's too quiet," Arjun whispers.

"Talk in a normal voice but a very low tone," you instruct. "It's even quieter than a whisper."

"Ironic," says Arjun, copying you. "Whisperers who don't whisper."

"It's conceptual," you say. "Quiet is good, right? Quiet means we won."

"No," Arjun says. "If we won, Sandhya'd be hollering orders right about now."

Your heart sinks as you realize he is right.

"It's all right, Krishi," he says, tugging the end of the long banner where it trails off your arm. "This is the part you're good at, right?"

You straighten up, buoyed by Arjun's words. But it's time to address your suspicion.

"Arjun," you say. "If we're going to do this, I need to trust you completely."

He is silent.

"You're him, aren't you? You're the missing King of Albahr. The reason you're 'missing' is because Dev Acharya brought you here."

Arjun inhales in the darkness and then blows out his breath. "Yes, Krishi. I am he. I am the King."

Your whole body relaxes and for the first time since all of this started, you feel confident. You feel believed in and confident. "I can get us through this, Arjun. The plan is going to work. All we really need to do is give Sandhya time and space, right?"

"Right," he says, firmly.

"So you follow my lead precisely. We do it exactly the way I said."

You approach the top and reach forward in the dark. There is a thick, heavy curtain blocking out all light. You hear the faintest sounds of shouting beyond it.

"I know where we are," you say in a low tone and slowly pull the curtain aside. Light floods in, and the two of you creep out as quietly as you can. You emerge from behind a heavy tapestry of the brilliantly shining suns that hangs below the mighty beacon.

Sandhya and the senior students are ranged along one of the parapets, their backs to the ocean. Before them, on the cobbled courtyard between the ramparts and the beacon's pedestal, are the Narbolin soldiers, their pikes pointing at the Whisperers.

You nod to Arjun, unrolling the banner and pulling it taut between you. You advance slowly, eyeballing the backs of the Narbolins' knees. You lower the banner a fraction. You both pause, coiled and ready. Sandhya catches your eye, but her face does not betray any flicker of a change. *Now that's a professional,* you think with admiration.

With a flick of your finger, you give Arjun the signal and you both sprint forward, pulling the banner as tight as you can. When it strikes the backs of the last row of soldiers' knees, they yell out a cry and suddenly Sandhya's arms fly up and she shouts a syllable you can't hear. You feel the banner being pulled forward with a force far beyond what you know you are creating. The soldiers collapse in a confused heap, and Sandhya and her students shout a battle cry and leap into action, subduing the soldiers.

"My goodness," she says, coming over and clapping you on

the shoulder. "Krishi, that was brilliant! They really had us there for a moment."

You bow your head to her in profound respect. "It was—" you gesture toward Arjun, not even sure what to call him. Sandhya's eyebrow arches in surprise.

"It's Arjun, Krishi. I'm always just Arjun to you."

"And who would you be otherwise?" Sandhya asks innocently.

"It's all right, master Sandhya. I've told Krishi."

Sandhya tilts her head in a way that implies she does not completely approve. "I trust Krishi," Arjun says, with some defiance.

"So be it," she says briskly. "Let's get this lot secured and then send word to Suraj and the younger children that all is clear." She fixes Arjun in her gaze. "I take it that yon pirate fleet is not going to have much interest in continuing a blockade now that their employers are, shall we say, guests of ours?"

"If they insist on continuing the blockade, I suppose we can always meet—or exceed—the Narbolins' price," Arjun says blandly, and you break into a wide smile.

"Good," Sandhya says. "They've had a long journey, I imagine. I'll send a messenger to invite them to supper. There is a lot to talk about."

"It happens that there is," you say in agreement.

THE END

SECTION 99

"I think we should try. If she's in there, she might be able to sense us and guide us in. And if she isn't, then at least I know I can keep you safe in there until all of this is over."

You start down the hallway and Arjun follows you. You force your mind to stay focused only on Sandhya, and finding her—now.

As soon as you make the first turn, you catch the slightest ripple in the rock, as if it were liquid. You know you are still in the Citadel—you can tell by how cool it is—but the hallways that open up before you in different directions don't seem like they could actually exist in physical space. Maybe it's your mind that's being affected. You've never been able to figure out how to navigate the maze. It's where all the levers of power in the Citadel are pulled.

As you take one turn after the other, you begin to think you have doubled back on yourself, but the hallways continue stretching away in the darkness.

"What's wrong?" Arjun asks.

"We're in it," you say. "We're in the heart of the maze."

You huddle together, Arjun's eyes glittering darkly in the faint blue light that illuminates the ghostly hallways.

If you think it is smarter to wait in the maze until Sandhya guides you, go to section 100.

If you want to continue to try to solve the maze, go to section 101.

SECTION 100

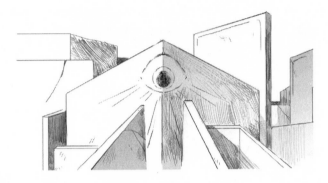

"She'll find us," you avow, as much to convince yourself as Arjun.

But the hours roll by and there's no hint of Sandhya, either mentally reaching out for you or physically in the labyrinth.

"Krishi," says Arjun despairingly, "what do we do now?"

And though the paths before you are many, you don't know which to choose, and you start to realize with growing dread that no matter which path you choose, none will lead you to freedom.

THE END

SECTION 101

Your mind reels. The paths before you seem infinite. You look from left to right, trying to decide which way to go.

"Krishi?" Arjun asks, hopeful yet fearful.

Your eye catches an engraving at eye level. A swirling cloud. You step closer. An eye.

The inner eye. Realization dawns. The Inner Eye.

"It's the dance," you say excitedly.

"What dance?" cries Arjun, jumping to his feet.

"A dance we learned in class. The Dance of the Inner Eye. Its steps are in a pattern: left-left-left-right. Right-right-right-left. Left-right-left-right."

"Show me!" Arjun says. "I'll follow you."

You head off to the left passage and follow the pattern of the dance. Each time you make a turn, you feel more and more convinced that you are making a right decision. When you make the final turn, you see sunlight streaming across the opening. You breathe a sigh of relief and you feel Arjun relax as well as you step from the maze into the light. With a shock, you realize it's evening already.

You hear Sandhya's voice shouting orders, and suddenly Suraj comes up the stairs with Dimple, one of the littlest students. "Krishi, thank the crescent! We didn't know where you were!"

"Krishi was keeping me safe," says Arjun simply, and Suraj relaxes visibly. He passes his hand over his face. "I'm sorry, we were all so worried."

"It's all right, Suraj," you say. "We're safe." You turn to Arjun. "Isn't that right, Your Majesty, King of Albahr."

Arjun smiles at you. "You guessed."

"You're not very good at being undercover."

"I'll learn."

Suraj says, "You two come with me. Sandhya's locking down the Citadel and interrogating the prisoners. It's time to find out exactly what the Emperor is planning."

THE END

SECTION 102

You approach the solar barque. As you draw near, it flares with golden light. You both place your hands on either side of it. The warm wood grows hotter and hotter. The light glows brighter and brighter until there is a sudden burst, and you feel yourself spinning through space.

Suddenly you are on the ground again, in darkness.

"Where are we?" asks Arjun.

"It's a staircase," you say, feeling around and ahead of you. "A spiral staircase." You know there are many such hidden thoroughfares in the Citadel.

"This is somehow *not* what I expected from a boat that is supposed to bear one sunward," Arjun mutters.

"We have to go up," you decide. There is actually no other way to go. You climb up the staircase. At the top a heavy black curtain hangs, blocking out most of the light. You think you know where you are.

You push aside the heavy curtain and walk out onto the ramparts. You look back at the curtain and see it's a heavy tapestry of two golden suns. It always hangs at the base of the pedestal where the beacon stands.

Go to section 10.

SECTION 103

"Let's get out of here," you say, carefully closing the cabinet and clicking the padlock shut. "We can't handle this alone. The most important thing is to get this information back to the Farmhouse."

"But what about our horses? We can't get them, and it will take forever to get back to the Farmhouse without them!"

You stop, thinking for a moment. You hear Meghan singing. She comes through the back door, swinging a wooden bucket.

"Oh, hello!" she calls out. Meghan rings the dinner bell and, to your alarm, everyone starts assembling in the yard. Tommy and Rubio move a long wooden table from the end of the yard. The men bring benches that were against the building and place them on either side. Max and Meghan bring dishes, serving spoons, and pots full of food from the kitchen.

"We take our meals under the stars," says Meghan gaily.

You and Saeed take your seats with the others, keeping your eyes fixed on each other. How are you going to get out of this one? Doron sits down on one side of you, and Max is on the other.

"Max," you say, using Saeed's trick of speaking out of the side of his mouth while his lips and teeth are closed. "We need some help."

"What kind of help do you need?" Max asks, using the same technique, all while serving himself some of the buttery cornbread Meghan has passed him.

"Do you think you can talk with me the other way?"

I can try, you hear Max think.

We have to get out here. Now.

Max looks down at his hands. Then he looks up and says, "Daw, I want to get more water out of the well. We need more."

Rubio blinks, looking down the table at Max. "Maxie, there is water right inside the house, no need to go to the well!"

Meghan is looking from you to Max, her eyes a little unfocused. "Oh!" she says, as if she's just remembering something. "Max, as long as you're going into the house for water, maybe you can take our young friends up to the ridge to look at the moon?" She looks at you and makes a tiny gesture with her head.

"Yes!" you say. "That would be great! Come on, Sahadev," you say to Saeed, who has just taken a big mouthful of cornbread.

"Yesh," he mumbles through the cornbread. "We'll be right back."

Max leads the two of you into the house.

"Now what?" Saeed says, panicking. "We can't just leave! Our stuff is in there and our horses! Oh," he adds, groaning and rubbing his belly, "and our food."

"We can't go back," you say. "This is our only chance."

"Be careful of the snakes," Meghan calls out. "And come back soon before the food gets cold!"

Max leads you silently out the back door, along the narrow space between the house and the canyon wall to the enclosure where the chickens are clucking. He pulls back a loose piece of fence and gestures you through.

"This trail leads all the way to the top of the ridge. When you get there, go west about fifty feet and there is another trail that leads down through a crevasse to the beach."

"Thank you, Max," you say fervently.

"You aren't coming back, are you?"

"We are going for help," Saeed says. "Can you handle things until we get back? Just keep going as if everything is normal. If they ask you where we went, tell them we didn't want to work and we ran away."

"We can't leave him," you say, coming to a decision. "Max, it's too dangerous. I think you are going to have to go with me and Saeed."

You expect him to protest, but Max nods solemnly. He understands more than you think.

When you get to the place where the crevasse opens onto rocky beach, you light the powdery stone the Duchess gave you and wait by its purple-tinged white flame. Before long, a long-boat pulls up in the dark. It's Zara!

"Ahoy, Krishi! Are you calling for rescue?"

"We've got an extra passenger with us," you say, gesturing to Max.

"Always room for one more," says Zara, looking Max up and down. "All aboard!" she calls out, the three of you embark, and the crew rows you back to the waiting lights of the *Blade*, from which notes of the Duchess's mournful tune drift across the water.

THE END

SECTION 104

"There isn't enough time to go for help," you say. "We have to stay and figure this out on our own."

"Okay," says Saeed seriously, all business. "What's the situation?"

"Five men. Big. Strong. Might have hidden weapons."

"Resources?"

You cast your eyes around the kitchen. "Besides the weapons in this cupboard, there might be some knives here? We have the element of surprise. We can choose the battleground."

"Wild cards?"

You take a breath.

"Max," you say together.

"All right," says Saeed. "Best strategy?"

"I think if we act with the element of surprise, and if we can get Max on our page, we can take them."

"Any potential liabilities?"

"The family," you say, exhaling. "I don't know which side of this they're falling on. Are they afraid? Or are they getting paid to hide these weapons? Maybe we're not going to do them any favors by taking care of these guys."

"It's a tough call," agrees Saeed.

If you think it's better to take down the men, go to section 105.

If you need more time to formulate a plan, go to section 106.

SECTION 105

When Meghan comes in to ring the dinner bell, you and Saeed spring into action. You snatch a bolo from your pack and Saeed improvises a blackjack with a doorstop and a sock. You hide your weapons under your shirts.

While Saeed helpfully assists Meghan in taking the dishes and serving pots out to the yard, you do a quick scan of Meghan's herb pots.

"Sleeproot," you mutter, sprinkling a pungent crushed leaf liberally into the soup bubbling on the hearth. "That should keep you nice and calm."

By the time dinner is served around a trestle table that Tommy and Rubio dragged into the center of the yard, you are tensed for action. You force yourself to make small talk with Rubio, who answers you with brief, curt sentences, while Saeed engages Meghan. The men mostly keep to themselves, though they joke with Tommy. You both eat with gusto, but studiously avoid the soup.

Suddenly Max says to you in a quiet voice, "I know what

you're planning." You glance over to him without taking your eyes off Rubio.

"What do you mean?" you ask, not moving your lips.

"I saw you put that leaf into the soup."

You take a chance. You turn to look at Max and think as hard as you can in his direction, *Are you going to help us?*

Max nods imperceptibly.

One of the men yawns noisily. "Meghan, you make an amazing cornbread!"

"I put honey in it," she says modestly.

"Daw," says Max suddenly. "There is something wrong with the pump in the house. I think we need to draw water out of the well to clean up tonight."

"What?!" Rubio exclaims. "I just fixed it this morning. Are you sure?"

Meghan stands quickly. "I'll go draw water," she says.

"I'll not hear of it," says Rubio. "There are panthers in the canyon at night."

"I'll take two of the men with me," Meghan says, gesturing to two of Doron's crew. The men grumble, but rise to accompany her. "You take a look at that pump in the house. And take Tommy with you to help," she says meaningfully.

Better odds, you think.

After clearing the table, Meghan goes off with two of the men, and Rubio and Tommy go into the kitchen to look at the pump. You are left at the table with Saeed and Doron and the last two men. They will discover quickly that there is nothing wrong with the pump. It's now or never.

"Where are you guys from?" you ask Doron.

He looks up and opens his mouth to answer. With all your might you upend the table.

Doron and the other men fall back in surprise, crying out.

"Now!" you shout and launch over the table, spinning on its edge and hitting one man in the side of the head with a front roundhouse kick. He goes down into the dust and you shuffle along the table's edge.

Saeed crawls along behind the table and rolls onto his back, kicking out and catching the other man. It's the same dragon kick he used back at the Citadel. Doron's man falls across the table edge and gasps as the wind is knocked out of him.

"Saeed, look out!" you call, as Doron lunges for him.

"Yikes," Saeed yelps as Doron catches him by the ankle and drags him a bit.

Rubio and Tommy cower in the house, frightened, but Max runs out into the yard, brandishing a shovel.

You run to help Saeed. The two men who left with Meghan run back into the lit yard, Meghan on their heels, her eyes wild with worry.

Max clonks the winded man with the shovel, and he rolls off the table edge and is still.

You run toward the two men who have just come in. Meghan meets your eyes and then takes her wooden bucket and upends it on the head of one of the men.

"Nice work," you call. You pull out your bolo and throw it. The rope tangles around his ankles and he goes down.

"*Arrrgggh.*" You hear a strange gasp behind you. You spin around. Doron is holding Saeed up off the ground by his throat. Saeed's eyes are rolling back and his head sags to one side.

"Saeed!" you scream.

Saeed cocks one eye open and winks at you, then brings both hands up, his left hand boxing Doron's ear and his right swinging the blackjack. You hear a thump and Doron's expression goes slack. He sways on his feet for just a second before dropping to his knees, releasing Saeed, and then he slowly, as if relaxing into bed, slumps over.

Saeed wipes his hands together as if cleaning them of dust.

"People always underestimate me," he announces brightly. "It's the little ones you have to watch out for," he advises Doron's unconscious form.

Rubio and Tommy come out of the house slowly. The last man backs up against the toolshed, away from Max and his shovel and Meghan, now brandishing her retrieved bucket.

"Get some rope," you order. "First we tie this lot up, and then we get some answers."

"Thank you for saving us," says Rubio roughly. "There is supposed to be another shipment tomorrow evening. They bring them in to an inlet on the other side of the ridge from here, and down through the canyon trails. We have no choice but to help them."

"We'll get help," you reassure him. "You're safe now, and with any luck we can keep the weapons from the people who would use them against Albahr."

THE END

SECTION 106

"There are too many of them," you say. "We need to figure out a strong plan."

"Too many of who? A plan for what?" says Meghan from behind you. She has come in from the back passageway.

"Nothing, ma'am," says Saeed, smiling. "A plan for harvesting cacti, of course!"

"What's happening in here?" Rubio asks, coming in from the front yard. "When is the dinner bell? The men are getting restless."

"The boys were talking about a plan," says Meghan nervously.

Rubio's expression grows hard. "Who are you?" he demands. "I had my suspicions. Nakul and Sahadev weren't expected for another three days."

"We . . . made good time," you say, trying to think fast.

"Nakul and Sahadev are said to be twins," he says.

Saeed throws an arm around you jocularly. "We are twins! We're fraternal twins!"

"And what might you be doing, young one, with your hair

unbound? Using your hairpin to try to pop that padlock, were you?"

You have a sinking feeling in your stomach.

"Doron!" Rubio calls out. He turns back to you, his face filled with regret. "I'm sorry, my young friends. I really am. But I have to think of my family first. I have to protect them."

Doron comes into the kitchen, flanked by two of his men.

"They're spies of some kind," Rubio gestures toward you. "I trust you will remember my loyalty."

Doron smiles tightly and gestures to his men to detain you and Saeed. "Your service to Narbolis will be remembered, Rubio," he says.

You struggle, but you cannot break free. For the moment, you have run out of options.

THE END

SECTION 107

"I'll stay here and keep an eye on this lot," you say darkly, glaring at Meghan and her family. "We'll keep everything in order until you get back!"

"Casey and Finnegan, you stay here and keep an eye on things," Doron announces. "Alec and Caleb, you're with me. Supper will be in Albahr tonight, boys."

The men grumble, but they immediately begin hitching up a two-wheel cart and saddling their horses. You gesture Saeed into the farmhouse.

"Come here," you say, huddling close to him. "We have to keep Casey and Finn distracted. Tonight when we all go to sleep, we can jump them and tie them up."

Saeed looks past you in alarm. You whirl around and see Meghan standing by the hearth, frozen, a long wooden cooking spoon in her hand. You straighten up.

"I might have something," she says slowly, "that could help." She reaches for a bunch of dried leaves and crumbles them into the soup.

"Sleeproot," you say. "To knock them out."

You wonder why Meghan is so motivated to help you, but you thank her and don't ask any questions.

She nods. "It doesn't work right away. It will just make them very tired. Just don't you two have any of the soup either."

Dinner passes slowly, and you make small talk with both Casey and Finn. In spite of yourself, you grow to like the two friendly brothers who are clearly devoted to each other. But you must protect this family.

Meghan's husband Rubio brings out a little fiddle after supper and plays a jaunty tune. Finn begins singing in Albahri while Casey and Saeed caper about the yard in an improvised dance.

As the night grows long, Casey yawns. He looks over at Meghan. "Ma'am, we do appreciate you. I'm sorry about all this."

"Casey!" snaps Finn in warning.

"We're only doing what we feel is right for all of us, Ma'am."

"I know, lad," she says kindly.

"You can't think that," Rubio says harshly. "You can't really believe the Narbolins will leave us alone. Not when they're starting a war."

"It's not for us to say," Finn says. "But it's our best chance. You may not mind slaving away for the rich dukes and barons on the bluffs and in the city, but we farm folk from the inland want our freedom."

"Let's sleep now," Max suggests suddenly. He turns to look at his father. You can feel the pressure of Max's thoughts. *He's being clumsy.* What if someone notices they are being pressured? "Father, let's sleep."

The belligerent look on Rubio's face fades. He smiles. "All right, lads. Let's rest and be bright again on the morrow."

As the household retires, you wait. Once the last candle is out, you tap at Rubio and Meghan's door. Rubio throws the door open.

"Casey and Finn are asleep," you say. "Change of plans. The new shipment will be arriving shortly enough. We need to get out of here and bring reinforcements. There's a safe place not a few hours from here by horseback. If we lead the horses out to the main road we can be gone before these two know anything's afoot."

Meghan appears at Rubio's side. "The sleeproot in the soup will keep them sleeping, that's for sure; I put in extra." Her face softens. "And they'll not be blamed as much by their boss for being tricked by us this way."

Rubio agrees, and the four of you go to wake Max and his brother, Tommy. Before the moon is very high in the sky you are leading the horses up the canyon to the main road.

You'll be at the Farmhouse before dawn. Shivani and the Colonel will know what to do.

THE END

SECTION 108

"No," you declare. "The first priority here is to get Max back to the Farmhouse. The rules of our order are very clear about that. There's time enough for Shivani to send other agents to deal with Doron and his men." You turn to Max. "I'm pretty sure your family will be safe. They're too necessary to the Narbolins at this point."

Max nods. "I know the trails through the woods," he offers. "There's another crossing of Ribbon Creek. There's no bridge, but it's shallow enough there that you can wade across."

"Where?" you ask.

"Just about about a mile west of where our cart path meets the Creek Road."

You whistle. "That'll shave two hours off our journey on foot!"

That night, after the others are asleep, you all creep out into the yard. You spy the outline of Casey at the far end of the yard, standing watch near the old crumbling postern.

You look back at Saeed and Max. Max's face is illuminated

by the three-quarter moon. He raises a finger to his lips and then points to his right, turning and creeping in that direction. He leads you behind the shed and into the underbrush.

Move quickly, you hear Max think. *If we move quickly, he'll think we're animals and get scared. If we creep, he'll be suspicious.*

Smart, you think. Max will make a good Whisperer.

The three of you bolt through the underbrush and, as Max suspected, Casey starts in alarm, whirling first one way and then another, but he does not leave his post.

You emerge from the thicket onto the cart path, scratched up and smarting, but free. You sprint for the Creek Road and then Max leads you in the opposite direction from the bridge, between two giant trees to an outcropping of rock. The creek rushes on through the night, but you can see a series of stones that Max jumps nimbly across.

"Come on," he hisses, and you and Saeed follow, a little slower. Before long you are on the other side, and from there it is just over an hour's tramp up the road.

When the dark shape of the Farmhouse looms ahead of you, you sigh with relief. As you come closer, you realize you must have tripped some kind of enchantment, because a light goes on and Shivani appears, holding a lantern that emits a golden light from no wick you can discern. Her long hair streams around her shoulders and a night cloak is still belted around her.

"Who's there?"

"Master Shivani! It's Krishi!"

"Krishi! What happened?"

You introduce Max. "His family is in trouble, master. The

Narbolins are smuggling the weapons by bringing them into one of the smuggler's coves west of the harbor, and up through the canyon trails." You take a deep breath as fatigue and relief hit you. "They stash the weapons at the farm. I don't know where they are taking them, but it isn't through the Marketfair. I think they're taking them somewhere in Albahr."

"Albahr! We must alert Dev and Chandh Sahib at once!"

"There's more, master. Max has Whispering talent," you say, gently pushing Max forward.

Master Shivani turns her piercing gaze to Max. You feel a subtle question emanating from her, but it is so delicate a gesture you cannot listen in.

"I am ten years old, Ma'am," Max says in answer to Shivani's unvocalized question.

"Now answer me the other way," says master Shivani out loud. This time you cannot even sense her gesture, but you do hear Max thinking inside his mind to her: *My mother's name is Meghan.*

Shivani smiles a broad smile. "I remember her! You never knew your Maw was a Whisperer, did you, lad?"

Max shakes his head in wonder.

"Good! She remembers how to keep a secret! You have done well and earned your supper. The Colonel made turnips and greens tonight! You'd better get some sleep. There is much to do in the morning."

THE END

SECTION 109

"The Duchess is out there," you say firmly. "If we can figure out a way to signal her, we can catch Doron in the act and put an end to all of this. It's too great a chance to pass up."

"All right," Saeed says unhappily.

"Saeed, you stay here at the house to handle anything if the other men wake up. Max will need to lead me up the canyon trail to the cove."

You and Max sneak out the back door of the kitchen and along the alleyway leading behind the house and up into the canyon trails. Though there is a little moonlight to see by, you feel disoriented as Max leads you higher up the ridge.

As you round a corner, you trip over something and fall hard on the trail. Max yelps beside you, but is quickly muffled.

"Well, imagine that," drawls Doron from the darkness beyond the path. You push up and look toward the sound of his voice. He steps out into the light and you see him holding Max, his hand roughly over Max's mouth. "And what are two little cactus-pickers doing sneaking around so late at night?" His tone is joking, but his expression is hard.

"We were," you say, pausing to think, "just coming out to look at the moon."

"The *full* moon, perhaps?" he asks, his voice dripping with malice. "Who are you? Not some farmworker named Nakul, I suspect."

You close your mouth and remain silent. The rules of your order are clear. You must never reveal yourself. If you are ever caught, you must take your punishment.

Doron shrugs. "Your silence speaks for you. Whoever you are, you will not stop Narbolis tonight."

You crouch low, getting ready to fight. "Stay behind me," you tell Max.

Doron draws a long, skinny knife from his sleeve. "How fast do you reckon you can get to me?" he asks you, casually. "Before or after I can sling this blade into your little friend Max?"

"You wouldn't hurt a child!" you exclaim in alarm.

"Wouldn't I?" Doron purrs.

Your shoulders slump. You can't take the chance that he would hurt Max. "What do you want?" you ask.

"With you? Nothing. Run along home. But Max and I have a lot to talk about, don't we, little man?"

You gulp in surprise.

"Run back to your masters, Nakul, or whatever you want to call yourself. Tell them I have your friend and we're on our way to see the Emperor. I imagine he'll be very interested in learning all the secrets Max has to tell."

Max shrinks against you, but the knife-wielding Doron seizes him by the wrist and yanks him to his side. You stand, defiant, your fists clenched at your sides.

"I like your spunk," Doron concedes. "It'll take me an hour to reach my ship. That gives you a two-hour head start back to wherever you came from before I send someone after you. In the interest of our past friendship, I'm going to strongly suggest you put those two hours to good use."

He doesn't have to tell you twice. *I'll come back for you. I'll find you,* you promise Max silently.

I know, he thinks back. *Go. I'm not afraid.*

You turn. You run.

THE END

SECTION 110

"All right," you say. "We stay. We'll figure something out."

The next day passes uneventfully. Alec and Caleb return from Albahr. You and Saeed work with Tommy and Rubio in the thickets harvesting prickly pears all day, and in the evening you return exhausted, eating your meal with the others. There isn't much time to think of a plan, but you know you are at least keeping Max and his family safe.

The next morning, as Rubio readies the sacks for your day of work, you quickly consult with Saeed. "We've got to move on this. Tonight we need to try to stay awake so we can figure out how the weapons are coming in."

As you are saying this, Finn wheels into the yard astride a black horse, followed by Casey, riding his little donkey. "It's happened," he calls out to Doron. "There has been an insurrection in Albahr and the Narbolin forces have occupied the city."

"What of the King?" cries out Rubio.

"The King has been captured. He was hiding in some kind of monastery on an isle across the water to the south."

The Citadel! you realize. As you quickly sort through some of the heavy thoughts around you, you have a second realization: *Arjun, Arjun was the King. Dev brought him there for protection.*

"And the monastery on the island?" you ask, worry growing in your throat.

"Also occupied by the Narbolins," says Doron. "Those monks will pay for their treachery. According to Albahri law, the King abdicated when he left the territorial land of Albahr. There was a new election, and Lowelia, the Baroness of Two Rivers, was elected the new Queen. She signed the Writ of Accession."

"That's it, then," says Rubio, his shoulders slumping. "We are citizens of the Empire now."

THE END

ABOUT THE ILLUSTRATORS

ANDREA ALEMANNO was born in Naples, Italy. He grew up between books, sun, sea, and a lot of paper. He is an illustrator who always needs to fill a space with lines, preferably at 300 DPI. He graduated from the Academy of Fine Arts in Macerata with a degree in graphic and multimedia design and then received a further degree in illustration. He moved to many cities around Italy searching for new ideas. Now, three decades later (and a little bit more), he's still drawing and learning something new every day. In these years his works have been selected for several awards: shortlisted at BCBF 2021, iJungle 2019 and 2020, IBA volume 7 and 8, Annual of AI, Lucca Junior 2020, and his first picture book *Barchetta* was shortlisted at the "Premio Letteratura Ragazzi di Cento" in 2013, winning the bronze medal. He's currently working for Italian and international publishers, in picture books, YA books, and board games, both as an illustrator and as a cartographer.

IRIS MUDDY is a forest pond creature and freelance visual development/concept artist living in Spain. Her curiosity for expressing life's beauty, stories, and adventures is what drives her. Her favorite activity is enjoying the outdoors on bicycle or on foot.

ABOUT THE AUTHOR

KAZIM ALI was born in the United Kingdom and has lived transnationally in the United States, Canada, India, France, and the Middle East. His books encompass multiple genres, including the volumes of poetry *Inquisition, Sky Ward*, winner of the Ohioana Book Award in Poetry; *The Far Mosque*, winner of Alice James Books' New England/New York Award; *The Fortieth Day; All One's Blue*; and the cross-genre texts *Bright Felon* and *Wind Instrument*. His novels include the recently published *The Secret Room: A String Quartet* and among his books of essays are the hybrid memoir *Silver Road: Essays, Maps & Calligraphies* and *Fasting for Ramadan: Notes from a Spiritual Practice*. He is also an accomplished translator (of Marguerite Duras, Sohrab Sepehri, Ananda Devi, Mahmoud Chokrollahi, and others) and an editor of several anthologies and books of criticism. After a career in public policy and organizing, Ali taught at various colleges and universities, including Oberlin College, Davidson College, St. Mary's College of California, and Naropa University. He is professor and chair of the Department of Literature at the University of California, San Diego. His newest books are a volume of three long poems, *The Voice of Sheila Chandra*, and a memoir of his Canadian childhood, *Northern Light*.